BACKHAND

GOLD HOCKEY BOOK 2

ELISE FABER

BACKHAND
BY ELISE FABER
Newsletter sign-up

BACKHAND

ACKNOWLEDGMENTS

I have to send a heartfelt thanks to Jena, my beleaguered (and thoroughly awesome) cover designer. She's patient and amazing and I can't thank you enough for always seeming to understand my muddled ideas for a cover and making it into an eye-catching and gorgeous piece of art. I couldn't do this without you! Thanks for listening and reading my millions of emails! ;)

I also have to thank Jaci and Johanna who help me keep the Fabinators (my fan group) running and my Fabulous Fabinators themselves for being my sounding board, always showing me support, and pimping out my books. I so appreciate you!!

And to my editors for changing my books from steaming piles of ellipses and dashes and typos into a palatable story for you guys.

Who I absolutely adore! Thank you dear readers for getting this far and sticking with me and supporting my stories. I love you guys.

Last, my family, my boys, this journey I take is because you make it possible. Thank you for supporting my dream and for encouraging me when my words aren't flowing and my stories seem contrite and silly. I love you so much!

-XOXO
E

Owen and Noah, you both inspire me to do my best.

GOLD HOCKEY SERIES

Blocked

Backhand

Boarding

Benched

Breakaway

Breakout

Checked

ONE

Sara

THE LIGHT WAS PERFECT . . . until it wasn't.

Sara glared up at the large, brick-wall style shadow that was marring her perfect view.

Did the person not understand just how *freaking* long she'd had to wait for the moon to peek out from behind the fog, to gild the rotunda at the Palace of Fine Arts and reflect off the water in perfect symmetry?

She clutched her pencil—the same one that had been sketching furiously just seconds before—and leaned to the left, trying to get one more glimpse of the scene, to commit it to memory before it was . . .

Gone.

Son of a—

"I know you."

The male voice was chocolate ice cream with hot fudge and marshmallow fluff, warm sand sifting between her toes, the perfect ending to a dramatic rom-com all rolled into one.

The hairs on her nape rose, and she shivered, wanting to snuggle into the sound, to pull it close like a cuddly sweatshirt—

At least until alarm flared to life, and she remembered she was totally alone.

Suddenly, skulking around the Marina District in the middle of the night seemed like a horrible idea.

Her sketchbook fell to the ground, the book light that had been clipped to the top making a sickening crack as it hit the concrete and went out. She blinked, trying to get her eyes to adjust, but darkness descended as fog swallowed the moon back up. She gripped her pencil like a knife and held it threateningly . . . or at least as threateningly as a pencil can be held. "Back off."

Her attempt at a growl, a warning.

And not a very scary one at that, if the man's reaction was anything to go by.

A soft chuckle was the only thing she heard before the pencil was plucked from her fingers. Sara opened her mouth to scream, but instead of jumping her like she'd half-expected, he sank into a crouch and handed the pencil back.

"You shouldn't be out here by yourself," he said.

"Noted," Sara muttered and shoved it into her pocket before bending to grab her sketchbook and light. "And you shouldn't ruin a perfect setup."

A flash of white teeth penetrated the darkness. "Noted," he said and put a palm to his knee, as though to push himself to standing.

Her eyes dropped. They'd adjusted enough to see his hands. And those hands were *gorgeous*. Long, lean fingers and neatly trimmed nails with enough character to make them interesting. She flipped to a blank page of her sketchbook, flicked the switch on the light, and spread his fingers on her thigh. The contrast, the shadows, the scars on his knuckles. His hand was the perfect juxtaposition and she *had* to get it on paper.

"Umm—"

"Shh." Her pencil flew across the page. It made a soft scratching sound as she worked, outlining, shading in the image, blending and building until his hand was captured on paper.

She didn't know how long she worked, just that when she'd finished, her neck ached and her legs were stiff and . . . a strange man had his hand on her thigh.

Her breath caught, and she looked up.

He was beautiful. Oddly familiar with his face half-illuminated in the lamplight, eyes as dark as ink, several days of scruff on his cheeks and chin, nose just slightly askew, as though it had been broken a time or two. And was that a bruise just above his right cheekbone?

Sara didn't have a chance to look closer.

His fingers flexed on her thigh, and every one of her thoughts beelined straight for that particular body part. She was in jeans, so it wasn't like he was touching her skin. But he might as well have been.

The warmth of his palm seeped through the thick material, made her quads flex. He was huge, his hand spanning the width of her thigh easily, and just the kind of man she liked. Big and strong, tall and wide-shouldered. Here was a man who could do all the clichés: protect her, shelter her, weather proverbial storms.

"You done?" The soft question held just the slightest hint of amusement, except there was a bite to the humor, as though that piece of his personality hadn't been used in a good long time.

No. She wanted to sketch his face, flip his hand over and draw the lines of his palm, but she'd submitted enough to her artist-crazy for the evening. And her hand was sore.

"Yeah," she said, ignoring the slightly breathless quality to her voice and standing.

Sketchbook into her pack, light off and into her pocket, stiff and aching hip, ribs, and shoulder from sitting too long on the cold, hard ground. Yup. All was as it should be.

The man stood as well. His size on the ground hadn't done his real breadth justice.

He. Was. Ginormous.

Okay, so she was petite, barely five feet three, but this man towered over her.

Yet she didn't feel scared. Embarrassed, maybe, that she'd hijacked his hand for—she pulled out her phone and glanced at the time—an hour and a half. But definitely not scared.

And she'd focus on that at a later time. For now, she should probably make an escape before she looked even more crazy cakes.

"Sorry I messed up your sketch," he rumbled.

She nibbled on the side of her mouth, biting back a smile. "Sorry I stole your hand for so long."

He shrugged. "My mom's an artist. I get it."

Well, there went her battle with the smile. Her lips twitched and her teeth came out of hiding. If there was one thing that Sara had, it was her smile. It had been her trademark in her competition days.

Which were long over.

Her mouth flattened out, the grin slipping away. Time to go, time to forget, to move on, to rebuild. "Thanks," she said and extended a hand.

Then winced and dropped it when her ribs cried out in protest.

"You okay?" he asked, head tilting, eyes studying her.

"Fine." And out popped her new smile. The fake one. Careful of her aching side, she shrugged into her backpack. "I've got to go." She turned, ponytail flapping through the hair to land on her opposite shoulder.

"That—" He touched her arm. "Wait. I *know* I know you."

She froze. That was the second time he'd said that, and now they were getting into dangerous territory. Recognition meant . . . no. She couldn't.

There had been a time when *everyone* had known her. Her face on Wheaties boxes, her smile promoting toothpaste and credit cards alike.

That wasn't her life any longer.

"Thanks again. Bye." She started to hurry away.

"Wait." A hand dropped on to her shoulder, thwarting her escape, and she hissed in pain.

"Sorry," he said, but he didn't release her. Instead, he shifted his grip from her aching shoulder down to her elbow and when she didn't protest, he exerted gentle pressure until Sara was facing him again. "It's just that know I *know* you."

No. This wasn't happening.

"You're Sara Jetty."

Her body went tense.

Oh God. This was *so* happening.

"It's me." He touched his chest like she didn't know he was talking about himself, and even as she was finally recognizing the color of his eyes, the familiar curve of his lips and line of his jaw, he said the worst thing ever, "Mike Stewart."

Oh *shit*.

TWO

Mike

SARA *FUCKING* JETTY.

Mike watched the horror cloud Sara's face, drawing her brows up and her mouth down. Even in the near dark, he watched her skin go ghostly white.

"It's been a long time, Jumping Bean."

Her head jerked up at the old nickname, and that horror turned to anger. He understood why. Didn't mean he liked it, though.

"I need to go." She whirled away.

"Hey. *Wait.*"

She didn't, just took off along the path, not running exactly, but definitely not waiting either.

Which didn't matter. Because he was taller. And faster.

He caught up to her in a couple of strides, snagged her elbow, and, careful to not hurt her again, tugged her to a stop.

He expected to catch up with her, to be able to stop her from escaping. What he didn't expect was the shit fuck of a crocodile-death-roll she pulled on him.

Sara spun, struggling in his hold and probably bruising her arm to hell and back. "Let. Go."

Jesus. "All right. Fine." He released her, raised his hands in surrender. "I was just trying—"

"I know all about men *trying*," she muttered. "Just leave me alone."

"Christ, woman. It's been ten years. I only wanted to find out how you're doing."

"You're kidding me, right?" she asked, brows practically in her hairline.

Why did he suddenly feel like this was a trick question? "Uh. No."

Her arms flopped down to her sides, and Mike was reminded of how small she was. Her backpack straps practically dwarfed her shoulders, and she was still so dang short. Put-her-in-his-pocket, Teacup-Poodle-in-a-world-of-Great-Danes short.

"You have to be kidding," she snapped, "because you cannot possibly be serious about asking me how I've *been*."

Okay, now Mike was starting to get pissed. Here he was, trying to be nice, trying to catch up with an old friend, and she was being a total bitch. He ignored the voice in his head telling him that he should really know what she was talking about.

"Sweetheart, I haven't got a clue what you're spouting off about," he growled. "So either tell me what's up or answer the damn question."

"I've been fucked, Mike. Royally and permanently fucked. *Okay?*" Whipping around, she started stomping away.

What the hell did that mean?

"Sara—"

"Oh. My. God." Her feet skidded to a stop, and she threw him a dark look over her shoulder. "Just leave me alone. This isn't like when we were kids. You can't fix it, you can't fix *me*."

The weight of those words hit him in the gut, stealing his air more effectively than getting checked into the boards on the ice.

And by the time he recovered, she was running, running down the path that led to the street.

Running straight out of his life.

Damn, was that a familiar feeling.

NOTHING WAS BETTER than being on the ice. *Nothing.*

The way his skin went tight when the cold hit it, the crunch beneath his skates, the sounds—laughter, pucks colliding with the glass, pinging off the goalposts, the Zamboni rumbling to life. He even loved the smell.

Akin to wet asphalt after a rain, there was already the slight odor of moisture in the air, not in a bad moldy way, but in the best hours of his childhood.

Escape. Friends. Camaraderie.

Family.

"Looking awfully introspective for a hockey player, Stewie," Blue, the rookie, said, using the new nickname the boys had decided to bestow upon Mike, mostly because they knew it drove him nuts.

"Rookies who tease better watch themselves," Mike responded, his tone falsely threatening.

Blue wasn't exactly a rookie, not any longer anyway. He'd had a phenomenal season the previous year that had him in the upper echelon of NHL stat charts—sixty goals, thirty assists, and a gritty, tough-as-shit work ethic.

"Good thing then that I'm not a rookie." Blue grinned, not intimidated by Mike in the least. The kid had always had way too much confidence, but they were at a better place this year.

Namely, Mike had burned his asshole card and started acting like a good teammate.

He bumped his shoulder to Blue's, and Blue, thinking he was returning the friendly gesture, leaned in to do the same. But Mike scooted away, just enough that Blue was off-balance, then dropped his gloves and stick.

In a flash, he had Blue's jersey up and over the kid's head.

"Still a rookie in some ways," he said, patting him on the back, grabbing his gear, and skating away.

"Oh look! A present!" Brit shouted from the net. "For me? *Aw.* Mike, you shouldn't have."

Blue wrestled with the fabric encasing him, pulling it down and knocking his helmet askew in the process.

"Fucker!" he called, but he was grinning, and so were the rest of the guys.

Family.

Mike hadn't thought it possible, but somehow the shit in his life had settled, and he'd found his family again.

Then he thought of Sara, running head down, shoulders bowed through the street, and his grin faded.

THREE

Sara

THE BELL to the shop tinkled as a customer pushed through, but Sara didn't bother to put her pencil down. She'd worked at the gallery long enough to know with a simple glance if a person was buying or not.

And this one wasn't.

Then the bell jingled again. Her eyes flicked up, and her pencil hit the paper. She straightened and tried to look professional when a well-dressed man came in and approached the counter.

He was hot, had a body like Jason Momoa, and he was . . . her boss.

He also, unfortunately for the female population, wasn't straight.

"Sara, honey," Mitch said, leaning over the artfully cut piece of granite to buss her cheek. "I've told you before, I don't care if you draw while you work, honey."

He had. Many times, but Sara couldn't just put the oh-God-her-boss-is-looking-at-her fear aside. She'd never been friends with her teachers or coaches because she had a problem with authority.

Namely with always bending to its will.

"Pathetic," she muttered.

"No, you're not," Mitch said fiercely, and her eyes flew up to meet his. "You're talented and sure as shit shouldn't be working behind the counter of my shop." He bent close, his voice softening. "Hun, your stuff should be all over my walls."

Sara let her gaze slide away, tracing the display of metal sculptures in the store's windows. They were good, way more intricate than anything she could ever come up with.

Then again, her strength wasn't sculpture. It was pencil sketching.

"My stuff is fine. Nothing inspirational, nothing amaz—"

Her words cut off as he snatched the sketchbook from beneath her hands and strode over to the older gentleman, the not-buyer, who was now perusing a set of postcards. Mitch flipped through pages as he walked, stopping on a drawing of the Golden Gate Bridge.

The sketch was her favorite, though probably not her most technically sound, with the swirls of shadow and light, her version of the notorious fog curling around the span, creeping over cars and pedestrians alike.

Done all in shades of gray, it had only the barest hint of the bridge's famous coppery red.

"What do you think of this?" Mitch asked the customer.

Sara's throat closed up, sweat broke out on her forehead, and her heart absolutely galloped in her chest.

The man's eyes went wide, brows climbing almost to the wisps of white hair sparsely covering his shiny scalp. "That's amazing," he said, his voice soft and practically breathy. He raised a hand as though to touch the image, and Sara winced.

Mitch slid it out of reach. "How much would you pay for it?"

"Is it an original?"

"Yup."

"Two grand."

Sara's heart was no longer galloping. It had stopped, frozen in her chest, along with every other part of her body.

Mitch laughed and put on his master negotiator hat. "It's worth three times that."

"I'll give you four." The man pulled out his wallet.

"Fifty-five hundred," Mitch countered.

"Five."

Mitch glanced over at her for the first time and raised a brow. She read the unspoken question in his expression. Did she want to sell?

For five thousand dollars? Hell *yes*, she wanted to sell.

Approval slid across Mitch's face. "Sold," he said, and they began talking about framing and matting options.

And in the span of five minutes, she'd sold her first work.

Holy balls of Satan.

She might actually make a go of this artist thing.

Later when the store had closed, Mitch handed her a check for the drawing. She blinked when she saw that no commission had been taken out.

He tapped her on the nose before she could protest. "First one's on the house, sweetheart. Just make sure to save something for taxes."

Her eyes filled with tears.

"None of that," he said. "I know you've had a shit time of it, but things are going to get better. I promise."

Oddly touched, she pressed a kiss to his cheek. "Thanks, Mitch."

"Give me some more drawings to sell, and that'll be thanks enough."

The thought made her nervous, but she gave a determined nod, shoved her sketchbook into her backpack, and shrugged into her coat.

Sara called her good-bye and left, thinking the world might be just a tad bit friendlier than she'd previously thought.

Of course, she was disabused of that notion exactly ten minutes and three blocks later when the skies opened up.

It was February, smack dab in the typical rainy season of Northern California, and the downpour shouldn't have come as a surprise.

The weatherman had even predicted it. And gotten things right for a change.

Unfortunately, her umbrella was currently sitting in Mitch's office.

Well, nothing to be done about it.

Tugging her hood up, she moved faster. Her apartment was a good nine blocks away, and since she was already soaked through, she might as well press on.

A car drove by, and she flinched away from the curb. Though it was too soon for puddles to have formed and for the tires to kick them up onto her, the instinct had been honed by five years of San Franciscan living.

She did *not* want whatever was in that water or on the street anywhere near her.

Her obsession with avoiding the nonexistent puddle was probably why she missed the car stopping. At least until the driver's window whirred down, and she heard Mike's voice, trailed by a cacophony of screeching tires and blaring horns.

"Sara," he said, calmly. As though he wasn't just chilling in the middle of the lane, as though cars weren't swerving around him and delivering fingers and curse words alike.

"What are you doing?" she asked.

Water streamed down her face, soaked through her clothes. She pulled her backpack off and clutched it to her chest, thankful it had a waterproof inner layer.

He raised a brow. "Want to get in?"

Mike Stewart, unwelcome blast from the past, professional hockey player, and former Mr. Popular of Nowhere, Minnesota, had parked in the middle of Market Street to have a casual road-side chat.

"Yeah, no," she said. "I'm cool." She started walking again.

The tires of his car made a whooshing sound as he trailed after her.

"What are you doing?" she shouted and waved a hand at the line of angry drivers behind him. "You're blocking traffic."

"Get in, Sara. We need to talk."

Yeah. That wasn't happening.

"No, we don't, Hot Shot."

"Sara," he growled, probably as much at the old nickname he hated as the fact that she wasn't obeying his orders, and kept pace with her. Which meant he was driving all of five miles per hour down the busy San Franciscan street.

The stoplight in front of his car turned red, and he slid to a stop. Not even Mike would blow a red light. He might have the same slice of reckless as every other member of the male populace, but he didn't risk other people.

Or he hadn't used to, anyway.

Which is why she wasn't getting anywhere near him. He didn't need to be mixed up in her garbage.

With a wave, she hurried around the corner, starting down a side street that would actually take her farther from her apartment.

But since it was a one-way street—the wrong way for

anyone particularly pesky and exceptionally annoying to follow
—she would be safe.

Mike had different ideas.

"Sara." He'd gotten out of the car and was right behind her.
And that voice, melted chocolate and velvet all mixed up in one,
slid down her skin. It stopped somewhere in the vicinity of her
lady parts. Damn. That intensity, the *alpha* inside him making
an appearance . . .

Shut it, haters. She could be a feminist and still like the
growly way the man ordered her around.

Liking didn't mean she was going to obey, after all.

Except maybe in the bedroom, or against the building, rain
sluicing down their faces, soaking into their clothes, cooling
their heated skin as Mike pounded into her—

And holy crap-on-a-stick, where had *that* come from?

The Mike she knew had been gangly with acne on his chin.
He'd been sweet and kind and . . . not interested in her in the
least.

Her Mike no longer existed. Which tended to happen when
more than a decade passed.

Straightening her shoulders, Sara turned around. "What do
you want?"

"It's been years, sweetheart. Last I heard, you're on the
podium with a gold medal around your neck. Then nothing. No
word, no email." His voice dropped, and she shivered, not in a
good way this time, since his gaze was pinning her in place.
"You just pop up in my city with demons in your eyes."

"I don't have demons," she said, taking a step back.

"Yes." He came closer, bent so his head was near hers.
"You do."

She opened her mouth, but he didn't give her a chance to
respond, just plucked her backpack from her arms and strode
back down the street.

"Hey!" she shouted. "Stop!"

He didn't.

"Mike! Wait!"

He tossed her a look over his shoulder, not stopping, not waiting, just walking away. "Doesn't feel good, does it?" he asked.

No, it damn well didn't feel good.

But then again, she'd had plenty of experience burying the hurt that came along with people walking away from her.

FOUR

Mike

MIKE TOSSED Sara's backpack into the passenger seat, dropped himself and his sopping wet suit into the driver's seat, and waited.

Five. Four. Three. Two—

Sara didn't disappoint. She wrenched open the door and reached for the backpack. "What the hell do you—?"

Yeah, not happening.

Mike snatched it up and gave her a look, waiting for her to sit down and close the door.

Her eyes went heavenward, and she sighed. "Can't I just—"

"No." He tucked the backpack down by his legs.

A horn blared behind them, jolting his mind back to the present, back to the fact that he was in the middle of Market during rush hour and had just casually parked his car in the right lane.

An SUV screeched by, its driver waving a certain finger.

Mike raised a brow. "Gonna get in, sweetheart? Or you planning on playing *Frogger* all night?"

Huffing, Sara collapsed into the seat, slammed the door, and glared at him. "Happy now?" she snapped.

Attitude.

He had to bite back a smile. At least that piece of her hadn't changed.

And neither had the fact that he liked when she gave him sass.

"Not yet." He slanted her a look. "You know the rules of my car."

"No seatbelt, no move," she muttered, snapping the belt. "Yes, I remember your caveman nonsense all too well."

"Good."

Mike turned off his hazards—traffic in this city meant people did way crazier shit than just blocking a lane—and shifted the car into drive, happy that the locks automatically engaged. The look on Sara's face was half-irritation, half-pure-terror, and he wouldn't have been surprised if she'd tried to launch herself from the moving vehicle.

"Where to?"

She was silent and after a moment, he shifted back into park.

Her eyes flashed to his.

"Where. To?"

Her lips moved, but no sound came out, and he could almost picture her mental count to ten.

Right about eight, he said, "I can do this all day, baby. You know I can."

Ice. Frosted spikes hit him in the chest. Directly in the heart. Or at least, that was what her glare said. She crossed her arms, sighed, and then gave her address.

Without another word, he took off.

The car was silent, not uncomfortable exactly, but it also

wasn't the easy familiarity of their youth when he'd driven her to their local rink.

They'd both had private lessons before school, Sara for figure skating, Mike for hockey. And since her parents hadn't allowed her to get her license until she was eighteen, and he'd been two years older, they'd had a lot of early mornings together.

"Remember the first time I drove you?"

She was quiet for so long that he thought she'd refuse to take the trip down memory lane with him.

But eventually her lips quirked up, and she smiled.

That smile took his breath away. It always had.

"Yeah," she said. "You weren't much of a morning person."

He stopped at a light, backed up and clogged with cars. People in California really couldn't drive in the rain. It probably also didn't help when assholes from Minnesota blocked traffic for diversions down one-way streets.

"No, I'm still not," he said, grinning at her, wanting to find some of their old camaraderie. "But you were."

For a second, he thought she wouldn't play along. Then her mouth curved. "I was nervous back then. I blab when I'm nervous."

"Nervous?" he asked. "Why?"

She snorted. "Because you were gorgeous and older and popular, and I was—"

He waited for Sara to finish the thought but was met with silence. Eventually, he settled for touching her cheek, shocked at how silky soft it was.

Her breath caught, and he saw something reflected in her eyes. Not desire exactly. Instead, it was more like . . . fear?

What did Sara have to fear? Especially with him?

The thought made him unreasonably angry. *He* was different. They were different together. Always had been and—

Ten years had passed.

He dropped his arm.

"How long have you lived in the city?"

"Why?" she asked, suddenly suspicious.

His eyes rolled heavenward, and he mimed a steering wheel. "Me drive. You small talk."

The wariness dropped off her face, and her eyes sparkled with amusement.

Sara had the best eyes, cat-like and slanted up at the corners, long lashes, and irises that were the clearest, deepest blue . . .

A car honked behind them, and he jumped, glancing forward and seeing the light in front of him turn yellow. He sped through just as it changed to red.

Ah well. His driving karma was certainly taking a beating today.

"So I have to confess I don't know where I'm going," he admitted as they pulled to a stop at the next signal.

Sara sighed. "Turn left ahead."

He did and followed the remainder of her directions until he pulled his car up to the curb in front of an older-looking building. A Chinese restaurant, a laundromat, and a watch repair shop, all with neon lights and peeling paint, took up space on the ground floor.

"*This* is where you live?"

She rolled her eyes. "Not everyone is a millionaire athlete, Mike."

"Last I heard you were on your way to becoming one."

Her shoulders stiffened and her chin came up as she met his stare head-on. Finally, she *looked* at him. Those cat eyes hit him like a fist to the gut, serious and holding a hurt that hadn't been there a decade before.

"You really *don't* know, do you?"

FIVE

Sara

MIKE SHOOK HIS HEAD, and Sara couldn't believe he hadn't heard, that he didn't know how violently her life had imploded.

For a few years, it had seemed like every person in the world knew her pain, that she'd become the poster child for unsportsmanlike conduct in professional sports. She'd been banned from the U.S. Figure Skating Association for life. She couldn't compete, couldn't coach.

The sport had been everything to her.

And then it had all been taken away.

Her purpose, her endorsements, her friends, her parents.

She was all alone—

Ugh. That didn't matter. She needed to shove that all down. Get over it. There was no going back to change the past. *This* was her life now.

Reaching over Mike, she snatched her backpack, holding it tight to her chest. "Google it."

"Google *what?*"

Raising a brow, she said, "I think you know what." Then she popped the passenger's side handle and slid from the car.

The downpour hadn't let up, and rain soaked through her shoes, wetting her socks. It dripped from her ponytail, trailed down her spine.

But she hardly noticed any of that, because the passenger side window rolled down, and she heard his voice.

"See you soon, Sara."

Not likely after he Googled her.

She turned and jogged for the stairs on the side of her building.

Later that night, she sat beneath the crappy light of the exposed bulbs in her studio apartment's ceiling and watched the San Francisco Gold play.

For the first time in years, she watched something with an ice rink in it, and while she'd felt a little jab at seeing the pristine sheet of white, hockey was different enough from figure skating that it was okay.

Or maybe it was because Mike was there on the ice.

His face serious, his muscular bulk even larger with the pads.

And he was magnificent.

Fast, strong, crafty, and creative, Mike was a master at defense. Paired with Stefan Barie, captain of the Gold, along with Brit Plantain in net, the first female goalie in the NHL—no big deal there, right?—and the team easily defeated their opponent.

Next would come their postgame routine—cooling down, meeting with the trainer, showering, and getting ready to do the same thing all over again the next day.

Sara couldn't deny that her heart ached for that routine. Not for hockey, as she'd never had the right temperament for the sport, but for competing. For giving every last drop of herself on the ice, skating until her quads threatened to give out, trying a jump—and trying and *trying*—and ending up covered in bruises only to crawl out of bed before the sun rose the next morning and getting right back out there.

For her, the sport was expensive skates and fleece-lined leggings, rolling bags full to the brim with Band-Aids and wraps and blister pads. The smell of the rink, the moisture in the air, the black skate mats, the left-behind water bottles from a kids' hockey practice the night before.

It was cold air tightening her skin, the crunch of the ice beneath her skates. Fogged-up breath clouding the air in front of her nose and mouth. It was—

—never going to happen for her again.

Not now. She was too old. She'd lost her chance.

"No," she murmured and scrambled for her notebook. Dutifully shoving those memories aside, she took the easiest way to numb her thoughts. The quickest and least dangerous.

She drew.

Except this time, it wasn't the architecture of the city, not the clean lines of skyscrapers mixed with Gothic peaks and curves of Victorian moldings emerging from beneath the point of her pencil.

Instead, she drew a sharp nose, stubble dotting a strong jaw, a scar bisecting one arched brow.

She drew—as she'd done too many times before—Mike.

HER ALARM CAME WAY TOO EARLY, and Sara spent the first half hour of her day muzzy and stumbling.

But same as she'd done since she was ten years old, she pulled on her workout clothes, did a short yoga routine, and went for a run.

The run was her favorite part, even though it was a lesson in pain management nowadays. The yoga she merely tolerated.

It made her bendy and all that jazz.

Not that she needed to be bendy. Not any longer at least.

Still, she ran because she loved it. Getting lost in the city, earbuds in and nothing but the sidewalk in front of her simplified everything else.

People didn't care about her past. Not here. They had jobs to get to, deals to make, tourist sites to see.

Running was easy anonymity.

An hour later, she'd showered and was walking toward the studio. Mitch didn't open the doors for a couple of hours, but Sara always got there early on Fridays.

It was shipment day.

Or basically Christmas and her birthday all rolled into an hour of awesomeness.

She let herself into the studio and made her way to the storeroom. Ryan, the delivery guy, was waiting outside the back door and helped her get the heavy boxes inside. After signing the shipment form, she spent a happy hour digging through the packages like a kid on Christmas morning.

Sara was just dragging a reclaimed metal depiction of Sisyphus pushing his proverbial rock up the hill—and boy, was that ever *the* metaphor for her life—from the storeroom into the studio, when she heard a knock.

She glanced up and was promptly assaulted by a stomach full of butterflies.

None other than Mike Stewart was standing outside the store's glass windows.

He waved when he saw her looking.

It really wasn't fair. No one had a right to look that good in jeans and a leather jacket.

He knocked again, pointed at the door.

For a second, she debated ignoring him.

Except, it was Mike.

If he'd parked his car in the middle of the street to chase her down, he probably wasn't going to let a pesky pane of glass stop him.

Dusting her hands on her pants, she walked to the front of the store.

Mike watched her approach the door and slipped through literally the second she'd unlatched the bolt, like he was afraid she was going to change her mind and lock it right back up.

She gave a mental shrug, thinking he had the right of it. Her impulsivity was almost as widely known as her downfall.

Once inside, he locked the door then swung to face her, his nose an inch from hers, his eyes holding her frozen.

They were furious, dark-brown depths that she half-expected to shoot sparks.

"Why didn't you fight it?"

Shocked by the force of his anger, she stammered out, "H-how did you know where I worked?"

Eyes narrowed. "I saw you come out last night as I drove by." He lifted a hand. "How, Sara? How could you—?"

She flinched, took a half step back. Not from his hand, but because she'd heard those words too many times.

Mike hissed out a breath and, instinctively, she jumped.

Very rarely had she seen him furious and *never* had she seen him like this. A cloud of black anger surrounding him, spilling into the space between them.

His hands came to her shoulders, his grip tight, and he jostled her slightly, made her teeth clink together. Her ribs and hip protested the movement, but she didn't tell him to stop. Some sick part of her felt the pain on the outside should match that within her heart.

Despite her intentions, Mike must have realized he was

hurting her because he dropped his hands, though his words didn't soften. "Sara, why in the *hell* didn't you fight?"

It all finally clicked, and she couldn't hold back her wave of disappointment.

He'd obviously taken her advice and Googled her. Knowing Mike had seen her like that—at rock bottom, broken, defeated— was almost worse than her going through it the first time.

The one person in her life whose view of her hadn't been tarnished and she pushed him to go ruin it.

Every emotion from those horrible weeks of her life flashed right back into the forefront of her mind.

Mike had burst the dam with his quiet demand, and it didn't matter to him in the least that she had reasons for wanting to bury that part of her, for trying to shove it all down and forget. He *wanted* to know why.

Icy calm flooded her veins.

It was better this way. Better that he knew now, that he hated her from the get-go. Certainly, it was better that any and all expectations were crushed before they grew too large.

Sara put her hands on his stomach, but it didn't feel good— those hard, flat abs certainly *didn't* feel good beneath her palms. She shoved him hard and took a couple of steps back.

Mike followed her.

"Stop. No," she spat when he took another stride in her direction. "I'm serious. This"—she waved a hand at the shop —"is my life now. Not skating, not the past. If I wanted to talk about that shit, I'd be seeing a therapist. Don't bring it up again."

She turned and snatched up a pair of scissors from the counter, then stomped into the back room.

"Sara."

She didn't respond, just got to work on the next box.

And suddenly he was there, crouching slightly so he could look her straight in the eye. "I just want to understand."

Her hands plunked onto her hips, and she winced when the scissors jabbed at her side. She didn't protest when Mike plucked the pocket-sized metal death trap from her grip and set it on a box.

She did, however, sigh. Everyone wanted to *understand*. Trouble was, no one wanted to believe what had actually happened.

"I don't have anything more to say about it."

"So you cheated? Paid off the judges for higher scores? Is that what you're saying?" He touched her cheek. "Because, Sara, I don't believe it. You wouldn't—"

Good. God. Men. Could. *Not*. Listen.

She pushed past him, strode over to the door, unlocked it, and held it open. "Out."

"No." He leaned against the wall just outside the storeroom, crossed his arms.

She resisted the urge to cross her own in return. "I'm not talking about it."

"You need to talk to someone about what happened."

Ha.

It took every ounce of her restraint to hold back bitter laughter.

When had talking *ever* solved anything for her?

"Been there, done that." She pulled her phone from her pocket. "Now go. Or I'm calling the police."

And there they were, staring each other down like they were on opposite sides of an old Western street, about to draw their guns and duel.

Sara surprised herself by not backing away from the challenge. She'd given in so many times over the years, but she didn't bend today.

That was something.

Lifting her chin, she held the door in one hand, the phone in the other, and waited.

And—surprisingly, shockingly, and a whole slew of other adverbs—Mike caved.

"Fine," he said, walking toward her. "No talk of the last decade. We'll discuss other things. Deal?"

She hesitated. Why was he here now? Why, after all these years, did he want to spend time with her? Why did he seem to care when no one else did?

"Sara."

Her eyes found his, and her heart skipped a beat at the gentleness in them.

"We were friends once." His voice was soft, kind.

"Yeah." They *had* been friends, aside from the fact that she'd had the biggest, most painfully unrequited crush on him.

"I'd like to be friends again."

It was scary, but she *liked* the sound of that. She was so tired of being lonely. Tired of holding everyone at arm's length. "You would?" she asked.

He flashed her that grin, the one that had turned her teenaged heart to mush. "Yeah." In two steps, he'd closed the distance between them and plucked her phone from her hand. "There," he said, pressing some buttons before handing it back to her.

She heard his phone buzz.

"Now you have my number."

All casual-like, he carefully pushed her aside and strode through the door, closing it behind him.

"Lock up," he called through the glass.

Numbly, her fingers obeyed.

"Talk soon."

And, hurricane in her life that he was, Mike was gone.

SIX

Mike

FLYING in a private jet wasn't awful.

Aw, fuck, Mike couldn't pull off humble. Or not very often anyway.

Flying in a private jet was awesome. Lots of leg room, bathrooms someone could actually fit in, direct flights, and no crying kids.

The only annoying people were his teammates, and since he was used to their particular brand of annoying, the flights were usually fun.

They were flying out of SFO, delayed by the fog as per usual, for the first stop on an extended road trip. Management tried to organize games so that the whole renting-a-private-jet thing was kept to a minimum in order to save money.

This leg they'd be playing against teams in Columbus, Chicago, Philadelphia, Boston, and New York. Then they'd have two nights off and play the Capitals down in D.C. before returning home to the West Coast for a stretch.

Playing that many away games in a row—being out of their

normal practice schedule, their typical routines for almost two weeks—was grueling, but it was the life, and it was exciting in a way.

Less exciting now that he was old as fuck.

Or at least old according to hockey standards. Almost thirty, and he was on the leeward side of his career, grizzled and scarred.

Okay, yes to the scarred—it was tough to keep a pretty-boy face in a sport with flying pucks, blades on feet, and sticks in sometimes temperamental hands. But he couldn't agree with the grizzled part. He was in the best shape of his life, playing the best hockey of his career.

He'd gotten past self-sabotaging.

He'd been cured of his very serious, life-threatening asshole condition.

Things were looking up.

Mike couldn't help but think of Sara. She was still tiny as hell, barely coming up to his chest. But something had changed about her . . . well, obviously a lot of things had changed. He was just hung up on the most noticeable one.

She'd become a woman. He felt his face tilt into a smile and knew, *just knew*, that his buddies were going to give him shit for the grin.

But what a *woman* Sara had turned into.

She was petite, yes, her face almost elfin with its small delicate features. But, that wasn't what had made his mouth go dry when he'd spotted her through the window bending over a box that morning at the gallery.

No, his body had perked to complete attention because of the rest of it. Curves for days, pert little breasts he wanted to try out in his hands, a heart-shaped ass that he somehow just knew would be firm enough to bounce a dime off, a flat stomach, and delicate ankles.

He was an ankle guy. Which was weird as fuck, he knew. But something about the little glimpse of skin beneath the cuff of a woman's pants, the hint at what was hiding beneath, turned him on.

Yes, he was a freak. And she wasn't his little Sara any longer.

She'd *never* been his.

Oh, yeah. There was that.

"Whatcha smirking about, Stewie?" Max. Resident funny man—at least *he* liked to think so—of the team and general shit-stirrer.

And commence the shit-*giving*.

"Your mom," Mike countered, bending to snag his earbuds from his backpack. The insult was old and overused, perhaps, but still a good one, given the spots of red appearing on Max's cheeks.

"Ha. Ha." Max slammed down into the seat next to him and began pulling things out of his backpack.

And by things, Mike meant enough toys and books and snacks to keep an entire flight full of toddlers busy for hours.

"Dude," he said when Max started powering up some sort of video game system on his tray table. Little plastic characters towered precariously on the flat surface. "You're an adult."

"Young at heart, old man," Max said, pulling out a controller and headphones. "I'm young at heart."

A piece of plastic—some sort of dragon-horned toy—fell off the tray and landed on his foot.

It stung. The fuckers were heavier than they looked. "God, Max."

"Just God is fine."

"You're not funny."

One side of Max's mouth turned up. Mike had seen entire Reddit posts devoted to that mouth when someone had screenshotted and printed out pages of comments and memes to hang in the locker room. No one had ever claimed responsibility, but his guess for the perpetrator was captain, Stefan Barie, because though the guy came across as clean-cut and nice as hell, he had a wicked sense of humor.

Multiple women had declared Max's lips perfectly pouty, expounded on his mouth being kissable enough to make their ovaries explode, sinful enough to kill them dead.

Regardless of the grand adoration from the opposite sex, at that moment Mike was thinking he might prefer a plane full of screaming kids to Max's mouth.

"I'm hilarious," Max declared.

Yup. Definitely give him the crying babies.

He bent and snatched up the toy, pulling his tray table down and plunking the little devil-horn-dragon thing onto the surface. "You are a *lot* of things. Hilarious not so much . . . unless that is, you're referring to your face. Which is definitely a lesson in comedy."

Max chuckled then nodded at Mike's tray table. "Thanks. I could use the extra space," he said and proceeded to fill the entire surface of Mike's table with more toys.

Good God. They'd just taken off, which meant he had four more hours of this.

He jammed his earbuds in, cranked his music, and hoped that Max would take the hint to just. Stop. Talking.

Max didn't.

Of course not. He prattled on about the game he was playing, going into way too much detail about the characters and gameplay.

Mike also found he didn't really mind it.

Especially since the eager way Max jabbered on reminded him of Sara chatting his ear off during their early morning car rides.

Not that he would admit *that* to Max.

"Why ya smiling, Stewie?"

"Because you're an idiot."

Max grinned. "Why were you late to the game yesterday? Thought Coach was going to scratch you. He was that pissed."

Max had been late to the usual pregame festivities because he'd driven Sara home.

Not that he was sharing *that* particular piece of information with the class.

He'd let Coach know, calling him after dropping Sara and he was back on the way to the arena. Surprisingly, Bernard had been understanding after Mike had explained the situation.

In the past, Mike would have said, *"Fuck it all,"* and shown up late, not caring if he was scratched or not.

Things were different now. He had more at stake. He actually wanted to do well.

But that wasn't any of Max's business.

"How is it you're a grown man playing a game designed for ten-year-olds?"

"Hey! The graphics in this . . ."

And Max was off, easily diverted as he talked about pixels and plot lines. Mike closed his eyes, tuned his teammate out, and wondered if there would be a text waiting for him when he landed.

SEVEN

Sara

SARA GLANCED down at the screen on her phone, trying and failing to ignore the little green box with a bright red circle in the upper right corner.

She'd seen Mike's text that morning, watched it appear on the locked screen of her phone. And she hadn't opened it.

Oh, she'd read it all right.

Read every single word.

Hey, Jumping Bean. How goes it?

Which was really nothing.

Except that it was Mike. All casual-like. All relaxed. As though the fact that he'd texted her hadn't made her heart threaten to pound out of her chest.

As though the last decade hadn't happened.

So his text just sat there, the red notification on her message icon glaring and guilt-inducing.

Because she hadn't responded.

It had been hours, and she had *not* responded.

And the Jerk-of-the-Day Award went to . . . (Cue her award show presenter voice here.)

Except what *could* she say?

What's up?

Too abrupt.

How are you?

So formal.

How 'bout those Niners?

She didn't even watch football.

Hopeless. Sara was utterly hopeless.

"You know just because you stare at it doesn't mean it's going to ring, right?"

She blinked, glanced up at Mitch's smirking face. "Shut up."

Mitch ignored her retort and pointed at a painting she'd unpacked that morning. "What do you think of the Prescott?"

She thought it was brilliant and, accordingly, had hung it dead center on the studio's most prominent wall. The lighting made the texture of the acrylics really pop.

"It's going to sell fast."

He nodded. "Yes, it is." One of his brows came up. "And you'll be taking that spot. So get something ready."

Dread. It poured over her in a tangible wave, prickling the hairs on her arms, twisting her stomach, causing sweat to break out on her palms, the backs of her knees.

"Mitch, I—"

"No excuses this time," he said. "I thought we were past

this. You're talented and the discomfort you have with your work is insane." He bent close, placed his hands on her shoulders. "You're an incredible artist, and you deserve to have the world know that."

The world was what she was afraid of.

"I-I can't."

"You will," he said, his tone somehow both gentle and firm at the same time. "If you want to keep working here."

The slice of betrayal burned.

She stepped back, snatched up her backpack. "I'm a good employee." Her chin lifted. "If you don't want me working here—"

"Ah, honey, that's not it at all." He started toward her, but she put up a palm to stop him. "I love having you here. What I don't love is that it's still holding you back. *I'm* holding you back. You shouldn't be selling paintings to idiots with way too much money and unpacking boxes of other artists' work." He pointed to the Prescott. "You should—you *deserve*—to be right there."

Her heart raced for the second time that day.

Sara couldn't deny that she wanted that too. But the risk—media attention, dredging through her past for the umpteenth time, barbed comments from her family, the people she considered friends—it was too much.

She could not go through that again.

"I know you didn't cheat."

Her breath hitched, and she froze.

Mitch had never mentioned her past. She'd assumed he hadn't known.

"I—" She shook her head.

"Have you met me, honey?" He smirked. "While there are plenty of gay men who don't love sparkles and music and dancing, I'm not one of them. *Of course* I'm familiar with figure skating. I just didn't expect to find out that a disgraced Olympic champion was a fabulous artist as well." He touched her cheek. "Is there anything you can't do?"

So, *so* much.

She'd been great at skating, naturally talented and a skilled show-woman. She'd excelled at giving soundbites, never failed to put together a spunky-yet-sweet answer to even the dumbest of dumbass questions, but *Mitch* had struck her mute. All she could do was shake her head and clutch at the straps of her bag.

"You're too honest to cheat," he said. "It took barely five minutes with you for me to know that." His mouth twisted into a sad smile. "It's just unfortunate the rest of the world couldn't figure that out."

She snorted. Now that was for damn sure.

"Yeah, I know," he said. "So, here's what we're going to do. You bring me something to sell on Monday, and you'll still have a job. You don't, or you decide you've had it with my dictatorial-push-you-out-of-your-comfort-zone days, and we'll just be friends."

He grabbed her coat, shoved it at her, and pushed her toward the door. "Because, honey . . ." He did a cheesy jig and sang, " 'You've got a friend in me.' "

She found her tongue. "Of course you'd quote a Disney song."

"And do it in a bad rendition at that." He smirked. "For now, take off early. Think about it. *Dooo it.*" The last was a whisper that made her lips twitch.

Sara had stepped out the door and was turning in the direction of her apartment, awkwardly shrugging into her jacket, when Mitch's voice stopped her. "And while you're at it, maybe respond to that text you've been staring at."

Her hand came up, starting as a perfect princess wave before transforming into a very particular one-fingered salute.

He just laughed.

"You know I won't let you fire me, right?" she called.

"I know," he called back. "Just like I know you'll bring me something fabulous come Monday."

Her stomach was in knots at the thought because she suspected he was right. Shaking her head, she turned and started walking.

"And Sara?" She paused, middle of the sidewalk, wind blowing, people pushing past her, as Mitch yelled, "Forget texting back. I know it's shocking in this day and age but just *call him!*"

EIGHT

Mike

THERE WASN'T a text waiting for Mike when he turned his phone back on.

Acute disappointment swept through him, even as he tried to convince himself that it was for the best. Sara didn't need his drama in her life.

"All good, Stewie?"

He glanced up into the deep brown eyes of Brit Plantain, star goalie, kickass chick, and general all-around woman-with-a-heart-of-*gold*, no pun intended.

She wore only a black sports bra and the bottom half of her equipment and looked as though she were a reflection in a funhouse mirror. Don't get him wrong, she was gorgeous and strong and super fit, but Brit was also very lean.

Pairing that with blocky leg pads and baggy goalie pants meant the funhouse mirror-effect was in all its glory.

Her blond brows pulled together, and Brit frowned. "Mike? You okay?"

He blinked and forced his eyes away. "Yup. I'm good."

"Then why are you staring at me like I'm a bug?"

Mike bent to tug one skate off. "Not staring so much as thinking."

That made her pause, made her glance at him like *he* was the bug.

He snorted. "I know. It's uncommon for me, but it does occasionally happen."

One toned arm came up to perch on her hip and, good God, did the girl have guns. She'd always hit the weight room just as hard as the guys, but, just saying, Michelle Obama would be jealous.

"It's a girl," she said.

A groan built up in his throat, but he shoved it down. Now wasn't the time to show weakness, to let on how close Brit was to the truth.

Because the amount of razzing he'd take for it—

He almost thought, *it wouldn't be worth it*, but the words couldn't even cross his mind. Not when he knew that he'd endure any amount of teasing for Sara. She'd always been that way, always able to invoke his protective instincts. His wants. Desires.

His phone buzzed at his thigh, and immediately Mike's pulse picked up, heart jumping around his chest like a teenager going crazy at a pop concert.

Heaven help him, that he actually knew who the hot current boy bands were, but between the rookies and Brit having a turn with the weight room stereo, his music knowledge had become a little more . . . diverse.

Which was so *not* the point—

Buzz. Again.

"Idiot," he muttered, and snatched at his phone, almost dropping it in his efforts to both answer it and conceal the caller I.D. as Brit leaned over his shoulder.

He swiped across the screen and put it to his ear.

One-half of Brit's mouth quirked up. "Sara, huh?"

"Shut up," he snapped.

"Um." Sara paused, asked hesitantly, "Is this a bad time?"

"No!" he said, way too loudly, given the way the entire locker room shifted its attention to him. Shit. "No," he said, softer. "This is a perfect time."

Her breath hitched. "Oh, o-kay."

Mike stood and walked out the locker room door. Well, he more tiptoe-stomped, tiptoe-stomped since he still wore one skate and his other foot was bare. Once in the corridor, he leaned back against the wall, careful to keep his skate's blade on the black protective mat.

Not that his edges mattered much considering the game was over, but dull skates were the bane of any professional hockey player, and old habits died hard.

"Hey," he said, shoving all of his extraneous thoughts aside.

"Hey," she replied.

Silence.

"I—"

"I—"

"You go," he said.

"No, you."

And more silence.

He finally got his shit together and broke it. "So, what did you do today?"

"I got fired."

"*What?*"

Sara gave a little chuckle. "Okay, not fired so much as threatened to be fired, but it's a good thing, I think—"

"Wait. What the heck are you talking about, Jumping Bean?"

She laughed, and it tinkled across the airwaves, slid down his spine like warm rays of sunshine on his back.

What in the *what*?

Now he was writing mental poetry?

But hearing Sara's laugh brought him back. It reminded him of the girl she'd been, the boy he'd thought he would always be.

It pulled him into the past. To a time when things had been so much simpler.

"I'm going to sell my work in Mitch's shop," she said. "Well, at least a couple of pieces and . . ."

"That's amazing," he said after she'd told him about the drawings she was working on.

"Yes." She paused, and he could almost picture her giddy smile, her white teeth biting into the blush pink of her bottom lip. "But that's why I'm calling actually. I wanted—um . . . I wanted to see-if-I-could-use-the-one-of-you," she finished in a hurry.

It took Mike a few moments to decipher what that rush of words meant.

But she continued before he could respond. "The one of your hand. Not the one of your face. I wouldn't do—I mean, I *couldn't* use that—"

For some reason, he was grinning. "You drew me? More than my hand?"

A muffled word that sounded very much like "shit," then Sara sighed.

"Yes."

"Was I clothed?"

"Mike!"

He laughed. He couldn't help it.

"Oh for God's sake," she snapped. "Yes, you were clothed. I — *Grr* . . . never mind."

Billy, one of the equipment managers, came around the

corner and started walking down the hall toward him. "Use whatever part of me you want, sweetheart," he murmured, pausing to nod at Billy as he moved past.

Her breath hitched. "Mike."

His voice dropped an octave lower. "I mean that, Sara. Anything of mine is yours. Always has been, always will."

"Mike!" she said, slightly shrill. "You can't say things like that."

"Why not?"

"Because that's not how normal people talk. We haven't seen each other for a decade. You can't just—"

"Sweetheart, I've never cared much for rules."

Sara snorted. "*That* much I remember."

"And I always say what I mean." Or he did with Sara. "You feel me?"

There was only the slightest hesitation before she whispered, "Yeah."

"Good. Now I'm going to finish changing out of my gear and when I get back to the hotel I'll call you, 'kay?"

He could hear her smile through the phone. "Okay."

"Good," he said again. "And Sara?" he asked before hanging up.

"Yeah?"

"I'm glad you called."

"Me too, Hot Shot," she said and for once the nickname didn't make him scowl. "Me too."

NINE

Sara

SARA TOSSED DOWN HER PENCIL, abandoning her sketch of the city's rooflines for the moment.

The work was a lost cause anyway, since instead of the jagged peaks of the Gothic building, she kept drawing the chiseled line of Mike's jaw, the hash marks of scars he had on his knuckles.

Groaning, she flopped back onto the carpet.

She'd been dumped into a parallel universe; that had to be it.

A universe where men actually cared, where old friends had faith.

Where she actually kind of liked the alpha-act that Mike was putting on.

Not that she thought Mike's alpha-ness was an act, per se. He'd always been the type of guy who was confident in his own skin, wholly comfortable with the man he was inside, the kind of person who just lived unapologetically.

The difference was more because she actually liked it when Mike got a little bossy with her.

And now she needed to tear up her feminist card.

Pathetic.

Except—and this was the big one—Sara was so damn tired of doing everything on her own. Of being so locked up inside that she felt nothing. Of having no one able to wield an axe large enough to smash through the ice surrounding her heart and . . .

She was lonely.

Her eyes flicked to her cell. It sat, screen darkened, on the floor next to her sketch.

The sketch of Mike's face, eyes laughing as he stared out from the paper, hand extended, waiting.

Waiting for her to take hold and—

Ugh. *She* was ridiculous.

And yet she couldn't get him out of her head.

With a sigh, she picked up the pencil and gave in. She sketched the lock of hair that fell across Mike's right brow, the tiny scar at the corner of his eye, the scruff he'd been sporting in the game earlier.

Because of course she'd been watching. She'd held her breath each time he'd made contact with another player. Cheered when he'd made a particularly good pass up to the rookie, Blue, who was on a hot streak and had taken it up the ice to score the game-winning goal. Winced when he'd blocked a shot.

Her phone buzzed, pulling her out of her revelry. Groaning, she stretched her aching neck. She was getting way too old to be lying on the hard floor for—her eyes flicked to her clock as she snatched up her cell—over an hour, drawing.

Her phone buzzed again, and she slid her finger across the screen, heart pounding at the sight of Mike's name there, before putting it up to her ear. "Hi," she breathed.

And mentally groaned. Good God, she sounded like a nervous little schoolgirl.

Pathetic.

"What were *you* doing?" Mike asked.

"What?" Her eyes flicked to the sketchbook, to her ridiculous collection—yes, it was now growing into a freaking *collection*—of drawings. "Nothing," she rushed to say and even to her own ears it sounded guilty.

Oh. Em. Gee. She flopped onto the rug, tapping the back of her head to the floor a few times, just for good measure.

Or rather, to knock some sense into her idiotic brain.

"Hmm." His voice had an edge of rasp, as though that scruff she'd seen on his face earlier was scraping against the inside of her thighs, sliding up, up—

Her breath caught.

"Something to share with the class, Sara girl?"

Oh for God's sake. She needed to get it together.

She cleared her throat—and clenched her thighs. *PG, woman. Keep it PG.* "I was just working."

"Oh." His tone went serious. "Did I interrupt? You can just hang up on me—"

And there her heart went filling with helium, floating in her chest, somehow resuscitating the piece of her she'd thought long dead.

"No," she said. "If I'd been engrossed, I wouldn't have answered the phone. I probably wouldn't have even heard it."

"I'm glad you did," he said. "And that you picked up."

She smiled and rolled onto her stomach, stretching out the kinks in her neck. "I've missed you."

For the last few days.

For the last decade.

He'd been her best friend. And then he hadn't.

Sara released a slow, steady breath because it wasn't until

he'd come back into her life, started to help her cast off the fog she'd been living in that she realized just how much she'd missed him.

Mike inhaled rapidly. Well, she heard a burst of noise that her brain identified as Mike sucking in a gasp of air. But before she could ask what was the matter, he spoke, and his words froze the breath in her lungs.

"Sure do like you saying that, honey."

Sweetheart. Jumping Bean. Honey.

When was the last time someone had addressed her with an endearment? Besides Mitch, that was, for whom honey and sweetheart and a plethora of other sweet nothings were as common as the F-word was for hockey players.

But the same words out of Mike's mouth . . . *whew*. Those words made goose bumps come to life on her arms, twisted her stomach into knots—in the *best* way—and caused her inner teenage girl to sit up and squeal.

The last was what finally brought her to her senses.

She pushed to sitting and rubbed her forehead. Why was she always so impulsive? Why had she said she'd missed him? "What are we doing?"

Silence. "What do you mean?"

Sara snagged her sketchpad and flipped to a new page. Her pencil was on the paper in nearly the next instant, forming dark and angry squiggles across the blank white space.

"I mean." *Scratch*. "What are we doing?" More lines. "We haven't talked in a decade." Smudge. "Now, we're just casually chatting on a Friday night?" Add shadow. "Running into each other on the streets?" Fill. *Scratch*. Smear. Erase. No. *Darker*.

"Sara." His tone held a note of warning, and the audacity of that pissed her off. He was warning *her*? Really? Yeah, not going to happen. "You've always been important to me," he said.

No. *This* was important. Finding out his ulterior motives for striking up a relationship with her here and now were even more so.

Hell, if she was so *important,* then why hadn't he even tried to keep in touch with her?

After she'd left, she hadn't received a single phone call. Not one email. Not even a friend request on Facebook.

The worst was that *she* had called, *she* had emailed and . . . nothing.

"Yes, Mike," she bit out. "I asked what we're doing."

"We're talking."

Her pencil lead snapped, and she tossed the useless chunk of wood to the side. After reaching up to grab another out of the jar she kept on her desk, she continued drawing, her words almost as furious as the strokes of her pencil.

Some distant part of her mind wondered why she was so angry, but it was easy to push that aside, easy to focus on the rage.

Pissed off was safer than being vulnerable.

"Don't give me that bullshit. Why now? Why not then?"

One more line and she'd finished the drawing. Almost with disgust, she dropped the pad and pencil.

Why hadn't she been good enough then?

Charged silence stretched between them.

Then Mike sighed. "Weren't you the one who wanted to forget the past? Why can't we just focus on the now and move forward with our friendship?"

"No," she said. Sara *had* to understand. If she was going to open herself up to Mike again, then she sure as fuck needed to know what had happened after she left. "If I was so important, why did you find it so easy to let me go?"

His laugh was a horrible thing, brittle and broken, jagged and sharp. "Easy? Fuck, Sara. Nothing about you leaving was easy, but—"

She waited for him to say more, and when he didn't, she asked, "But what?"

"Google goes both ways, sweetheart. I'd suggest you use it." She could hear rustling on his end and just knew he was thrusting a hand through his hair.

He only did that when he was really frustrated.

And that made her anger fade, regret sneak forward to make her heart hurt. Why was she pushing this? Why was she pushing him away?

For once in her life, why couldn't she just leave things alone?

But she didn't get the chance to take the words back, to try and repair their easy rapport from the previous minutes.

"I'll call you when I get home from this road trip, okay?" He didn't give her a chance to respond, just hung up the phone.

That *click*, the sudden loss of Mike's voice in her ear, sliced Sara clean through.

With a pained breath, she put the phone down then picked up her pad again.

"Well, you sure do know how to ruin things," she muttered, putting pencil to paper.

She drew until the sun came up.

She drew until she saw Mike's face on television the next night.

She drew until she passed out from exhaustion and his features were no longer on the paper but tattooed in her mind.

She drew to forget.

Except she didn't.

TEN

Mike

MIKE WAS in a hell of a mood. Three days had passed since he'd fought with Sara. Three days had gone by without her voice and smell and laugh and . . . *dammit*, she was right.

How had he managed years without her but now missed her after only a few days?

It made no sense.

Except that it had been easier to forget the last good thing of his childhood after all the upheaval of his late teens, easy to be swept up into the life of a professional hockey player.

And when his past had refused to be shoved away, he hadn't wanted to bring anything good into contact with it.

His family contaminated everything.

They were a scene from a cheesy sci-fi movie, a cloud of black sweeping through the air, engulfing everything in its wake before tearing it all to shreds.

His parents had almost destroyed him. He'd nearly let their bullshit destroy the one thing that made him happy.

Hockey.

So finally, he had his head straight. He'd thought karma had brought him Sara because he actually had his shit together for a change.

Little did he know what she'd been through.

Cheating.

How could anyone believe that of her?

Sara had been the best skater he'd ever seen. Effortless, graceful, beyond gorgeous on the ice. And her level of difficulty had rivaled the male skaters.

But her coach had admitted in a tell-all interview that he'd paid off the judges, that he'd done it on Sara's instruction, had even released video of Sara meeting privately with them.

That had been bad enough, but deniable. There hadn't been audio, the accusations were just that. But then the media had dredged up evidence of large cash deposits into sketchy off-shore accounts.

Yet none of those had done what Sara's own ability had.

Because the killing blow was her scores.

Which were higher than any other skater in history. Clearly, it had been because of the money, not because she was exceptionally talented.

Except, that wasn't true.

He could almost understand how someone who didn't know her might believe that. But her friends and family? The way they'd crucified her on social media and to the press . . .

Sara's fall off her pedestal had been abrupt and from an exceptional height. She was banned from competitive skating, both in the U.S. and internationally. She couldn't coach, wasn't even allowed to teach a four-year-old how to stand up on a pair of skates.

"Fuck," he muttered, shoving his feet into sneakers and popping his earbuds in.

The Gold were still on the road, would be for another four

games. Mike had arrived at the arena early. He'd played for the Philadelphia Flyers for a season, knew the ins and outs of their home rink.

Which was good because he needed to blow off some steam.

What he didn't account for was Brit and Stefan standing outside the visitor's locker room. Oh, he knew they came to the games early—initially separately and now that their relationship was out and proud, so to speak, they came together.

They each wore sneakers and had their headphones on. Ready to go. Except that they appeared to be waiting for him.

Mike paused, wondering what the hell to say. He'd been upset since the fight with Sara, but he hadn't gone off the deep end. Had his inner turmoil screwed with the team?

He waited for them to lay into him, but his teammates, hell, his *friends* didn't speak. Instead, Brit raised a brow at his hesitation, pushed past him, and jogged into the arena.

"Oh God, you're going to let her go first?" Stefan moaned, taking after her.

Mike shook his head, confused as he turned his music to blaring and followed.

It took him two-point-two seconds to understand Stefan's complaint.

Brit set a blistering pace, jogging up the stairs of one aisle, down the opposite side, then across a row and into the next section. Up. Down. Across. Over and over.

And, fuck, but she was fast.

Mike was sucking wind by the fifth aisle, almost ready to puke by the last, and Stefan was no better off. When Brit stopped after they'd made the full weaving circle of the lower bowl, both of them collapsed to the ground, chests heaving, breaths coming in rapid gusts.

Brit stood lithe and graceful as a ballerina, one foot calmly bent behind her to stretch her quad.

She wasn't even out of breath.

"How?" he gasped, yanking out his earbuds. They vibrated from the music still blasting in them against his shoulders, the rapid *pound-pound-pound* of the punk band he preferred.

"How what?" Brit switched legs.

"How . . . are . . . you"—he sat up, sucked in a huge breath, tried to steady his racing heartbeat—"not even tired?"

She smirked and sank down next to him, continuing to stretch like a pretzel with what also appeared to be very little effort. "You're listening to the wrong music."

Mike frowned. "What do you mean?"

"I mean"—she dropped her voice and glanced around, as though imparting state secrets—"your music sucks. Makes you run slow."

Stefan groaned and pushed up to sitting next to them. "Don't listen to her, Stewart. Remember that her idea of good music is Miley Cyrus."

He winced. Yeah, if he heard "Party in the U.S.A." in the locker room one more time he might blow chunks.

"Yeah," Stefan said, "knew you'd see it my way."

"Whatever, losers." Brit stood. "Just remember who runs faster," she called, heading back down the hall toward the visitors' room.

"But who can skate faster?" Stefan called back.

"I'm a goalie! I don't need to skate fast." Her voice was almost drowned out by the pop music kicking on in the locker room.

Mike chuckled and reached for his phone, pausing his playlist.

"You know we're here for you, right?" Stefan said.

In the past, Mike might have made some snarky remark about heart-to-hearts, and Stefan not really giving a damn.

But Stefan did.

In Mike's entire playing career, he'd never seen a more devoted captain. Stefan cared about every single person in the Gold organization.

Legitimately cared.

Mike hadn't believed it at first, had thought it was a superficial façade. And if there was one thing he hated it was liars.

Turned out, he'd been wrong about Stefan.

So instead of brushing off his captain, he told the truth. "I'm fucked up over a girl." He thrust a hand through his hair. "It's like high school all over again."

And his feelings, lust and love and frustration, were tangled up inside his gut. Pathetic, really, but there it was.

"This Sara?"

Mike cut his eyes toward Stefan who shrugged unapologetically.

"Brit," they both said simultaneously then grinned.

"Never seen you with a girl," Stefan said after a moment.

"Never been any but this one."

Stefan blew out a breath. "Well, fuck. It's that?"

Mike nodded. "Yeah."

"So why aren't you going after her?" Stefan bumped his shoulder. "Or did you already fuck things up?"

"Not really." He stood. Well, truthfully, he had fucked it up with Sara. Both then *and* now.

"Aw, shit man, that means yes. Well, I'm sure you can fix it. Turn on some of that Stewie charm." Stefan's lips twitched as he pushed to his feet. "It's got to be in there somewhere."

"It's not that easy."

"Why not?" Stefan asked. "You love the girl, you go after her."

Ha. "And it was that simple for you and Brit?"

He rolled his eyes. "Brit and I were different. We had

complications because we're on the same team, because she was the first woman in the league."

Mike nodded in agreement. It was the truth. "I know you guys had it tough, but Sara's had a bad run of it too."

Stefan froze, his blue eyes blazing with fury. Their captain was an easygoing guy, but mess with his teammates or someone he considered innocent or vulnerable, and the man did *not* mess around. "Did someone hurt her? Do we need to—?"

A noose Mike hadn't realized was wrapped around his insides loosened.

Stefan hadn't asked, "Did *you* hurt her?" Instead, he was ready to kick the fucker's ass. Or at the very least, hold the jerk down while Mike did the honors.

Unfortunately, Sara's problems weren't on so small a scale— not that he wouldn't give his left nut to break every bone in her former coach's body. But her issues were on an epic, global, very public format.

"I almost wish it were that simple," he said.

"Then what?" Stefan asked. "What can we do?"

There went that loosening again, the bindings on his lungs slackening, feeling as though he could truly breathe for the first time in years.

"I don't know," he said honestly, "because *my* Sara is Sara Jetty."

"Well fuck," Stefan breathed.

"Yeah," Mike said. "Tell me something I don't know."

ELEVEN

Sara

SARA STIFLED a curse when she stubbed her toe on something large and heavy that hadn't been there the night before.

"Oh come on," she muttered when her inner teenager giggled at the unintentional sexual innuendo and then thought, *That's what she said.*

"You're an adult, Sara. Act like one." She fumbled along the wall, turned on the storeroom's lights.

Then winced when they revealed the sight.

The room was packed, absolutely packed, with wooden pallets and crates.

A whining noise escaped her, and she didn't bother to berate herself for the un-adult-like behavior. "Ugh. Why Mitch?"

Today was Wednesday. Friday was shipment day. *Friday* she expected the storeroom to look like this.

This wasn't Friday.

And she was tired.

Really, really tired.

Ten days since her argument with Mike. Ten days since sleep had gone by the wayside.

The plus was that she'd drawn a lot. The minus was that she couldn't sell any of it, since everything was of Mike.

And so it was Wednesday, and she was a real-life version of a walking, talking zombie.

Red eyes, pale skin, shuffling steps.

"Ugh," she said again. Why had Mike come back into her life and peeled back the layer of numb she'd surrounded herself with?

Life had been so much more comfortable when she hadn't really felt anything.

But Mike had traipsed back into her existence and burst through her barriers, and now she was all exposed and uncomfortable and . . . shit.

The bell above the front door dinged, and she straightened, her ribs already aching in anticipation of dealing with all the boxes, before calling out, "This is fucked up, Mitch! You do *not* pay me enough to deal with the amount of shit packed into this room!"

And silence.

And—shit, shit, *double* shit—there was only *silence* in response.

Which meant she must have forgotten to lock the front door of the store, and a customer had snuck in early and—

"Always did have a mouth on you, Jumping Bean."

Every single cell in her body froze then rocketed to full attention, honing in on the voice, whirling her body in a movement so fast that ninjas would have been jealous.

Mike.

She couldn't hold back the breath of relief that slipped through her lips.

If she'd had a cartoon bubble over her head it would have read, *Thank-freaking-God.*

He hadn't left her in the past, hadn't decided she wasn't worth the trouble.

And Sara hadn't even realized that she'd been worried about that until Mike was in front of her, eyes cautious but hopeful.

"Hi," she whispered.

One brow rose. "Hi." He leaned back against the doorframe, crossed his arms. "What did Mitch do?"

A snort, a wave of her hand to the disaster zone that was the storeroom. "Umm. Basically all this wasn't here when I left last night."

Mike's gaze flicked around the space. "All of it?"

Her shoulders sagged, and with a sigh, she bent to open the first box. "Yeah. All of it." She tore the flaps open. "Mitch does nothing halfway."

"*That*, I can see."

"He has this idea for an online art store. Which would be great—" She pulled out a gorgeous glass vase and carefully set it beside her before pushing the paper in the box to the side and retrieving two more nearly identical pieces. "—if he bought reasonable amounts. Or we had the storage space available."

Sara picked her way through the room and managed to place the pieces in a velvet-lined niche of cubbies that was built into one of the walls. Which was already full and, even though they moved merchandise at a pretty good clip, it would take weeks to make room for the pieces that Mitch had ordered.

And they still had their regularly scheduled delivery on Friday.

Which she knew since the delivery company had confirmed the previous day.

Closing her eyes, she let her head flop backward and sighed. How her boss survived the business world was beyond her.

The sound of wood scraping against concrete had her eyes flicking open, her gaze whipping to Mike.

Who was bent over a pallet, shifting it to the side.

"What—?"

He shook his head. "Let me help."

"But—"

"If we shift the bigger pieces to the side and take out the little boxes in between, we can get more space." A grunt as he shoved the entire square of wood against the back wall. "Then we can stack the less-fragile stuff."

"But . . ."

Mike straightened, flexed an arm. And good God, what an arm it was. She wanted to bite into it like a drumstick.

Holy balls, Sara. Get a grip.

"I've got muscles, sweetheart. Put 'em to work."

That he did, but still, Sara hesitated. "Are you—"

Two steps.

That was all it took for him to get in her space, to tower over her, to crowd her back against the stack of boxes.

Except it wasn't aggressive . . . or well, it wasn't disconcerting. Hell, that was a lie. It was both. The really unnerving part was that she liked it. Liked Mike so close, wanted him to come even nearer. She wanted *nothing* between them.

Not inches. Not air. Not clothes.

Her lungs hitched, and desire shot straight between her thighs.

Mike as a teenager had been nearly impossible to resist. Mike as a man—strong, tall, muscles-for-days, not to mention the sexuality and confidence oozing out of every pore—and resistance was useless.

"You have a game tonight. I don't want you to be tired."

"You know my schedule, babe?" His flash of white teeth

made her stomach tremble. It also made her lean closer for a better look.

"Which is your fake tooth?" she asked, since she wasn't going to answer his question about the schedule.

Yes, she'd been watching the games. Yes, she knew that he was playing that night at home before heading to Los Angeles for their game against the Kings. Then they would be back at the Gold Mine—the fans' nickname for Reynolds Arena—for an extended home stand.

But come to think of it, knowing Mike had a fake tooth wasn't really much better than knowing when and where his games were.

Obsessed, meet pathetic.

Mike stared at her for a moment before reaching down and gently encircling her wrist. He tugged her hand up, tapped her pointer finger to the tooth one left from the center. "This one."

Sara might have been embarrassed that she was practically performing a dental examination, if not for the fact that his movements had the side effect of bringing her very close to his body.

She sucked in a breath, felt her breasts rub against his chest, and stifled a moan.

Her hand was suddenly on Mike's shoulder, her back firmly pressed against the wall.

And—*God*—he smelled good.

He had mint on his breath, the faintest hint of cologne on his body, spicy and wholly male.

She wanted to burrow into him, to wrap the scent around her like a cat.

She wanted him to press into *her*, to feel that body of his firmly against hers.

And maybe she wanted to climb him like a tree so she could slant her mouth across his.

"Sara."

His voice was gravely, and when she met his eyes, the need within them was enough to take her breath away, enough to finally spur her into motion.

Enough for her to say, *"Screw it."*

She rose on tiptoe, leaned in, and pressed her mouth to his.

Mike froze, but Sara didn't immediately back away. She'd dreamed about this, wished for it, hoped that it might—

Arms banded around her middle, a solid chest pressed tightly against hers, lips opened, and tongues tangled.

And it was . . . glorious.

Heat blossomed in her stomach, spread to her limbs, desire pooled deep and heavy and low.

Her other arm came up, wrapped around Mike's neck, and she tangled her fingers in the soft hairs on his neck. His hands slid, hitching under her butt, and pulling her closer to his mouth.

She was wrapped pretzel-style around his body and not giving a damn when the very loud, totally indiscreet cough came from behind them.

TWELVE

Mike

MIKE GAVE a mental groan and gently released Sara's legs, letting them slide down to the floor. He made sure she was steady before turning to face whatever asshole had interrupted them.

A tall man with shaggy dark hair, tan skin, and green eyes smirked from the doorway. He wore a fitted purple suit with brown shoes and a paisley shirt.

If there was one thing besides hockey that Mike knew, it was suits—because he had to wear so many of them for game days.

This man brought the suit game.

Sara slid out from behind him and crossed her arms, glaring at the man. "What is this, Mitch?"

Ah. So that was Mitch. The boss.

And he should probably be feeling guilty for potentially getting Sara in trouble at work, but the kiss—her lips, her moans, her lithe body in his arms—was everything.

Mitch cocked his head to the side, his gaze flicking between the two of them. "I'm thinking that I should ask you the same question."

"No," Sara warned. "Really, you shouldn't."

"Is this Text Message?"

Mike's brows raised, and he glanced over at Sara, whose cheeks had gone a little pink. "Text Message?" he whispered.

"Shh, you," she muttered before raising her voice. "Who he is doesn't matter."

Ouch, Mike thought. *Tell me how you really feel, Sara.*

"We need to discuss your ordering," she said. "There's not enough room for all this."

"I've secured a warehouse for the online items. They'll be shipped here for photographs, then picked up, and transported there." Mitch waved away Sara's words when she started to respond. "We'll discuss the details later." His eyes cut to Mike. "For now, I think you'd better tell the truth to Text Message here."

"T-truth?"

"Yeah," he said. "You know, like the fact that who he is definitely *does* matter, given that you've been moping around here for the last week and a half."

Mitch turned, paused. "More kissing," he called over his shoulder. "More kissing might soothe the sting of that one, honey."

And he disappeared into the front of the store. The phone rang, and he heard Mitch answer it.

Only after Mitch seemed to have settled into a long conversation did Sara move.

She rotated to face him, teeth nibbling on her bottom lip. Which made him want to kiss her all over again, not exactly the best thing in this moment, all things considered.

Who he is doesn't matter.

Yup. That sounded about right. *That* sentiment had been drilled into him plenty of times over.

"Mike," she said.

"Did you Google me?"

He'd surprised her with the turn in the conversation. "U-um. No," she stammered before lifting her chin, straightening her shoulders. "If you want me to know about your past, I figure you'll tell me."

He snorted. Women were confusing as hell.

"So why did you tell me to Google *you?*"

She sighed, shoulders slumping slightly. "Because it was easier."

"Easier for whom?"

"For me."

He shook his head. "And you don't want to give me the same courtesy?"

White teeth pressed into soft pink lips. "No. It's not that."

"Sara."

"Okay fine. It's stupid. I mean part of it is that I didn't want to hash it all up again. It was easier if you thought the worst and just left me alone." She took a couple of steps, sat on the edge of a pallet. "But I mean, I know it's not common knowledge or anything, but everything you read on the Internet isn't necessarily true . . ." Her words faltered for a second. "I didn't want to read something bad about you and ruin this picture in my head, you know?"

"Ruin something more than the fact that the boy who had been one of your closest friends ignored your emails and calls? That he didn't make an effort to talk to you for a decade?"

That he'd been in his own personal hell and unwilling to bring Sara into it.

She laughed, but it wasn't a lighthearted one. Hers was

broken, fractured slightly at the edges. "Yeah. I guess there's that."

He crossed the room and sank down next to her. "I'm sorry I put all that distance between us. I shouldn't have."

"That's true." She sighed. "But I guess what I'm saying is that I kind of understand you needing to."

The tension between them softened, and he finally asked the question he'd come to the store in the first place for. "Come to the game tonight?"

Given her reaction, Mike might have stabbed her with a hot poker. Sara went stiff as a board; her mouth dropped open in horror.

"I can't go to a *game*." After popping to her feet in signature Jumping-Bean style, she began to pace the room. "It's —rather, *I*—"

"You could sit with the WAGs, not be in front of the cameras at all."

She paused, her gaze darting back to him. "WAGs?"

"Wives and girlfriends. They watch the game from a suite. It's very private."

Her laugh was shrill, slightly hysterical. "Yeah, except that I'd be with the *wives and girlfriends*. Are you insane? The press would have a field day with this. *Cheating Figure Skater Dates Bad Boy Hockey Player*. It's like a fucked-up version of *The Cutting Edge*."

"And how do you know I'm a bad boy? High school, I was squeaky clean."

She froze. He pushed to his feet, came directly behind her, the fresh floral scent of her skin drifting up and teasing his senses.

"It's just an expression."

"Try again." He pushed her hair to the side, exposing her nape, and unable to resist, pressed a kiss there.

Sara shuddered, released a shuddering breath. "Fine. I Googled. But just a little."

He chuckled. "God, Sara. You never did make anything easy."

She whirled around. "So?" She poked a finger into his chest. "If I'm so difficult, why are you here?"

Catching her hand, he smiled. "I never said it was a bad thing, Sara girl. Sometimes the best things in life are the hardest."

That he knew from personal experience.

"I understand, Mike, but I still can't—"

He kissed her, unable to resist. He'd had his taste, and now he needed more.

So much more.

Lips melded, tongues tangled, his dick was harder than he thought physically possible.

And when he broke away, saw that her expression was glazed, that her blue eyes were blurry with passion, he wanted to take her mouth all over again.

Except, Mitch hollered from the front of the store. "Two more minutes, Sara. That's all I'm giving you. God knows I don't want to stumble upon a naked woman in my storeroom!"

Sara blinked, desire starting to clear from her expression.

And Mike didn't want to let it. He ran his thumb across her bottom lip, leaned in to press a kiss to her jaw. "Come to the game, sweetheart," he whispered into her ear, reveling in her shiver, in the hitch of breath slipping from her mouth.

"I-I can't." But the refusal was gentle. He could press this; he could get his way.

Except, he didn't want to manipulate her into accepting. He wanted her to come because *she* wanted to.

"Watch it from my house then," he said, tucking a strand of hair behind her ear.

"I—" Her hands fell slack to her sides. "That's not a good—"

"Please, Sara girl?" He gave her the puppy-dog look. The same one that used to work on her as a teenager.

Okay, so he took his previous thought back—a little manipulation never hurt anyone, especially when she would get the privacy she needed and he would get to have her in his house.

And just like before, his sad puppy expression worked.

"I— Dammit, Mike. Not the *eyes.*" She shut hers. "Okay, *fine.*"

THIRTEEN

Sara

SARA GOT out of the Uber and stared in shock at the house in front of her. Just outside of the city, it was tucked into a rare patch of green and surrounded by oak and eucalyptus trees.

A long walk led up to the house, a twisting row of stairs crawling toward a front door obscured from view of the street.

And directly in front of her was a large gate.

She swallowed, pulled her phone from her pocket, and approached the intimidating row of iron.

The keypad was easy to spot, and she plugged in the code that Mike had sent her. Silently, the gate opened, and she slipped through, waiting until it was completely closed again before she hiked up the staircase.

Muttering a curse when her body protested as per usual, Sara pushed the pain down and continued up.

Six years since the accident and her bones still ached.

But she was walking, running, jogging, drawing. Things the doctors had never expected her to do, so really life was looking up.

The daily pain was manageable. God knew she'd done it enough in her competing days—pushing through hurts, ignoring injuries, continuing on when it felt as though she couldn't do one more jump.

But that was different than the emotional pain. *That* hadn't been as easy to compartmentalize. It bled into everything, crept back in at the most inopportune moments.

So she focused on the physical. The physical she could deal with. The physical she could do something about.

With a wince, she climbed the twenty or so steps leading up.

Another keypad was by the front door, and she put in the next code from Mike's text message, waiting, listening to the *whir* of the lock as it rotated and clicked open.

The knob was oil-rubbed bronze, dark brown and beautifully crafted, but it was nothing compared to the inside of the house.

"Holy mother of God," she murmured as she stepped inside.

For a minute, she just stared at the huge space in shock. Then the alarm gave an ominous beep, spurring her into action. She closed and locked the front door before locating the panel just to the right and inputting another code.

Mike's house was like Fort Knox.

But she supposed there were perks to not having to carry keys or wrestle with a deadbolt, like her apartment. Half her morning workout was trying to get the damn thing open after she'd returned home from her run.

Mike had told her to make herself comfortable, given her carte blanche to explore . . . except, where to start?

The entry was huge, with vaulted ceilings and a spiral staircase. She could spy a kitchen behind the stairs with a sunken great room and a wall of windows beside it. On her right was the only wall she could see on the first story. A pair of double doors broke up the expanse of white, and when she crept forward to peek inside, Sara saw it was an office.

She meandered forward, slipping off her sneakers and tucking them near a side table, lest she track dirt across the pristine marble floors. Since the upstairs—hello, bedrooms—seemed too intimate, she bypassed the stairs and went into the kitchen.

A vase smack dab in the center of the huge island held flowers.

Her breath hitched, and her eyes filled with tears.

Daisies.

He'd remembered her favorite flower.

Sniffing, she walked forward to touch one of the silky soft petals and spotted the note.

DON'T BE SHY, *Jumping Bean. Snoop away. Eat all the good snacks in the fridge. And when you find a room you're comfortable in, make sure it's got a TV.*

We're on channel 723.

—Hot Shot

A GIANT GRIN. Her cheeks were actually aching from smiling so hard.

She traced a hand over the stone countertop. It didn't look like marble or granite, more man-made, like Corian. But it was a pretty gray and the cabinets were a bright white.

Little dots of color—of bright-yellow and pale-blue—were sprinkled throughout. A cookie jar here, a decorative plate there. The look wasn't masculine or something that she would have associated with Mike's personality. She suspected he'd hired a designer.

But the space was homey, somehow warm despite the white and all the stone, and Sara found that she liked it a lot.

She could almost imagine cooking a meal with him, laughing and jockeying for position around the stove. Or maybe sneaking down for a midnight snack, eating ice cream straight out of the container while perched on that gray countertop.

And . . . yeah. She needed to chill out.

They were friends. Just friends reestablishing an old relationship. That's it.

Friends who kissed with enough passion to out-flame a match to kerosene.

Aw crap.

But so what if she preferred his kitchen to the crappy one in her apartment? *Anyone* would.

"Idiot," she muttered, snatching her hand back from the countertop as though it had possessed the offensive thoughts and not her own brain. "Chocolate. I definitely need chocolate for this."

Glancing around, it took her a minute to find the freezer. A built-in panel disguised the drawer from view.

Thankfully, ice cream was inside.

Unfortunately, or maybe *fortunately*—at this point she was beyond confused—there was a note on one of the lids.

On the pint of Phish Food.

No. I didn't get lucky with the daisies. I remember all your favorites . . . and how I used to be one.
—H.S.

SARA BLEW OUT A BREATH, swallowed down the tightness that had appeared from Mike's thoughtfulness. But sweet baby Jesus, the man was *killing* her.

Especially when she saw the P.S. on the back of his note.

SPOONS ARE *in the drawer behind you.*

"GIVE ME A BREAK, MIKE," she muttered, not that it stopped her from opening said drawer and pulling out one.

After leaving the ice cream on the counter to get nice and soft, Sara went out the door in the great room and stepped onto a huge deck. Immediately her heart skipped a beat.

The view was absolutely beautiful.

The city was in the background, rooftops undulating over rolling hills, a red snake-light chain of brake lights visible in the waning sunshine. The deep-blue, almost-black of the bay encircled the chaos.

Her fingers itched to sketch the scene. To capture it exactly as she was watching it now.

But she hadn't brought her sketchbook.

Rookie mistake, Jetty.

Staring intently, she tried to commit the sight to memory to draw later. She did it even knowing that she would fail miserably.

She did it because her heart wouldn't let her do anything else.

Finally, Sara forced herself to turn away from the sight, and that's when she spotted it.

The sketchbook.

Her preferred brand.

The cup of pencils.

She crossed to them, took in the little square of paper tucked under one edge.

Do it. *But don't forget about the game . . . or the ice cream.*

Mike, the boy, had been dangerous to her heart, wrapping it around his finger with easy charm and a plethora of kindness.

Mike, the man, was devastating. He'd cut straight through her armor and transported her back in time.

God. She just liked him so much.

And so, with a smile on her face, she picked up a pencil and drew until the sun went down.

Despite his warning, her ice cream was soup when she finally returned back inside, sketchbook in hand, but Sara didn't mind, just used the spoon to fish out the good bits and then drank the leftovers like milk.

If this was confession time, she might have done that to her ice cream a time or a hundred before, but she'd be the first to tell anyone that it tasted just as good melted.

She rinsed the spoon, dumped the container, and managed to turn on the TV in the great room just as the puck was getting ready to drop.

Sara had never been much of a hockey fan.

The game wasn't in her heart. She'd always appreciated the starkness of a single skater on the sheet of white, the beauty of using the ice to her advantage, circles and zigzags to cover every inch. Hockey had seemed so chaotic in its place. So many skaters, so much noise, so many blades cutting into pristineness.

She'd seen her fair share of games growing up, but none had been like the ones Mike played now.

And she was able to find the beauty in how the players

threaded passes through the other teams' skates, landing them directly on their teammate's stick, how they roofed pucks over goalies' shoulders. The scenes were filled with chaos and hits and bursts of color traveling at tremendous speed.

It was a choreographed routine of eighteen players and two goalies—hopping boards, opening doors, jumping into the play even as the action didn't stop.

Sara found that she liked *this* version of hockey very much.

Or maybe it was seeing Mike on the ice.

Maybe he'd changed it for her.

She snorted. *Of course*, he'd changed it for her. She was in his house, watching the game on his TV, flowers and sketchbook on the island, and reliving his kisses from earlier in the day.

He'd changed *everything*. He wanted something she'd never expected to give.

Not again.

Vulnerability was akin to death.

And yet, Mike didn't make her feel vulnerable.

He made her feel cherished.

The first period ended, and the reporter grabbed Mike for an interview before he headed to the locker room.

The Gold were down a goal, and she watched as he deflected the pointed questions about Brit's play and whether or not she should have made the last save. Instead, *he* took responsibility for the play. He didn't pass it on to the defense in general either, but shouldered it himself, saying he needed to improve, needed to read the play better, needed to work harder.

Sara watched in amazement. The respect she felt for this man . . .

He'd handled the tough questions with aplomb, barely sweating—or rather he was sweating only in the physical sense, not the mental.

With a wink to the camera that felt decidedly for *her*, he headed back to the locker room.

She picked up the remote, heart suddenly pounding in her chest.

That old impulsiveness reared its ugly head as she clicked off the TV, stood, and left the room.

FOURTEEN

Mike

MIKE WALKED into his darkened house and felt disappointment course through him.

She'd gone.

Or, hadn't come in the first place.

With a sigh, he closed the door to the garage, locking it before setting his keys on the kitchen island.

Which was when he spotted the sketchbook.

His heart expanded like a balloon being filled with helium. He strode over to the freezer, saw the pint of ice cream he'd bought for Sara was gone.

Like some insane paparazzi, he peeked into the trash, grinning when he found the empty container within.

And though he probably shouldn't—his mother hadn't liked him looking at her drawings—Mike didn't have the strength to resist looking inside the notebook.

Sara must not care too much, right? She'd left it on his counter after all.

Gently, he opened the cover and flipped through the sketches.

His amazement in Sara grew with each turn of the page.

He might not know much about art, but it didn't take a genius to see . . . well, genius.

She'd somehow captured both the realism and whimsy of the city, turning the rooftops into scales of a sleeping dragon, traffic into the beast's tail. Then he turned the sheet over and the next held a perfectly rendered drawing of the Golden Gate Bridge being engulfed by ocean fog.

No wonder her boss wanted to sell her work. They'd both make a fortune.

He closed the book and walked to the fridge to pull out a beer. So Sara had come and gone.

The disappointment for her having gone home was there for sure, though it was tempered by the fact that she *had* come in the first place.

He wanted to play this carefully, to not push Sara too hard, but at the same time, he needed to push her enough that they actually moved forward. They'd both been hurt, but she'd always been it for him.

They were right for each other.

He knew that more now than even when they'd been teenagers, when he'd forced himself to not act on his feelings.

To not hold her back.

God, he wished he'd ignored his chivalrous side. If he'd stayed in touch, been there for her—

No. His drama would have just bled over into her life.

They needed to move forward. Together.

He grinned, taking a swig of beer. Now he just needed to convince Sara of that fact.

And figure out how to deal with the press when the news came out.

Which it would.

With a sigh, he finished his beer, rinsed the bottle, and put it in the recycle bin. He flicked the lights and checked the alarm was functioning before crossing to the stairs.

He was tired, but that was a good thing. It meant he was working hard.

Of course, part of that was probably from allowing Brit to lead him on a wild goose chase through the lower bowl of the Gold Mine. He'd been following her on her workout since Philly and still hadn't gotten any closer to catching her.

He probably never would.

But he'd noticed a difference on the ice.

Hence, the continued hamster wheel of Brit stairs.

Round and round they went, never catching up and not really minding in the least.

His distraction with Brit's locker room music from earlier in the day—*Backstreet Boys,* good God—was probably why he didn't comprehend the light in his bedroom.

He strode through the door and screeched to what was certainly a very comical stop, had anyone been awake to see it.

Anyone being *Sara.*

Who was curled up on his bed, one of his T-shirts dwarfing her, a blanket half-draped over her body and giving him a glimpse of one bare leg.

Holy. Fucking. Shit.

Mike blinked. Glanced away and back.

But no, Sara was still there. In *his* bed. Wearing *his* shirt.

Suddenly, he wasn't the least bit tired. He was hard and aching and—

The Sleeping Beauty—no *Goldilocks*—that was Sara stirred slightly on the bed. Mike whirled away, unsure if he should be looking, and caught sight of her clothes folded neatly on a chair in the corner of the room.

He had to walk by them on the way to his closet, and he couldn't even lie and say he'd accidentally caught a glimpse of her bra and panties.

No, he actually stopped and pushed her jeans aside, nearly groaning when he saw the matching black lace set folded neatly atop her shirt.

Sara was in his bed, in his shirt, without a bra and underwear.

He bit back a curse and walked through the door into his closet.

Unzipping his slacks was the hardest—yes, literally the *hardest*—part. Jacket on the hanger, pants and dress shirt in the dry-clean hamper.

One sock off. The other and—

Cool hands on his back.

"Christ!" Mike jumped and whipped around, almost knocking Sara in the face with his elbow. He'd only just been able to adjust, to shift his weight and not accidentally clock her, but it had still been a close thing.

"Hey," she whispered, sleep in her eyes and an impish smirk on her lips.

His heart had been pounding because she'd startled him and he'd nearly hurt her. Now it threatened to burst from his chest for a whole other reason.

Mussed blond hair, naked breasts barely concealed beneath cotton, long bare legs, pink toenails.

Fuck. Her toenails were *pink*.

The same pink he imagined the hidden parts of her were.

And imagining those hidden parts was not helping his control in the least.

"Hope you don't mind," she murmured. "I got tired waiting for you after the game." A fingertip trailed down his chest, his abs, slipped under the waistband of his boxer briefs—

He caught that naughty hand and pulled it free. Her skin was like silk beneath his palm, warm and sleep-flushed, pale with just the hint of a rosy tone. She was strawberries and cream, and he wanted to lick her up.

"You can be naked in my bed anytime you want, sweetheart."

"I'm not naked."

He brought her wrist up, pressed his mouth to the delicate skin there. "*Nearly* naked then."

"Mmm." She lifted her other hand, gripping his shoulder as she rose on tiptoe to whisper in his ear, "So why did you stop me?"

He kissed her neck. "Who said anything about stopping?" A nip of his teeth. "But we should probably discuss the circumstances."

Sara huffed out a sigh. "I don't want to discuss anything. You're sweet and hot, and we're together. No talking." She dropped back onto the balls of her feet, met his eyes, and the mix of need and confidence in her stare made his blood pulse under his skin. This woman. She was hot as hell.

Especially when she tugged the T-shirt over her head and said, "I want you inside me. I want you to give me multiple orgasms and then wake me up in a few hours to do it all over again. I want—"

Her words were hot, but his mind stalled on her breasts, all perky and bouncy as she tossed the shirt aside.

In one quick movement, he swept her into his arms and strode back into the bedroom. "I meant more like I'm clean, and I have condoms."

"Oh—*oh!*" She gasped when he tossed her on the bed and pinned her to the mattress.

He was moving too fast, taking advantage, but this girl had been inside Mike's head for more than a decade. He didn't have patience when it came to Sara. He wanted her, *needed* her almost more than his next breath. If not breathing meant that he could have still brought her pleasure, found his own when he was inside her, then he'd have gladly given up the ability.

"I'm on the pill," she said and bit her lip. "I was clean the last time I got tested. Admittedly, it was a while ago, but I haven't been with anyone since . . ."

"Good." He reached for the nightstand drawer, extracted a condom, and set it on the pillow next to her head. Birth control pills or not, he wouldn't risk Sara.

"Good?"

"Yup." A smirk as he leaned back on his heels and picked up her foot. In reality, she was tiny, significantly shorter and smaller than him, especially since she always seemed so much larger in his mind.

But it was hard to deny the evidence of her size when her foot was in his hand. He massaged the sole, her toes with that delectable pink polish, and could easily feel the delicate bones beneath the surface of her skin.

Fragile. She was beyond—

Her other foot stroked up the side of his calf, his thigh, his groin, coming to rest just a hairsbreadth away from his cock.

Hot.

She was so fucking hot.

One toe stroked along his length, base to tip, before she allowed her leg to drop to the side, knee bent and effectively exposing—

Fuuuck. The pinks matched.

Mike felt his control slip another notch and forced his eyes up to the ceiling. He thought about tsunamis and short-handed goals, about stick length—

So. Not. Helping.

"Hey, Hot Shot. Getting lonely here." His gaze snapped

down, and he saw Sara's hand trailing lower, drifting south. And
. . . *hell no*. He dropped her foot and dove for her.

His mouth plundered on its way to her center, nipping,
licking, kissing, until he reached the apex of her thighs. He
gripped her hips, spread her legs with his shoulders, and went
to work.

She tasted like cotton candy, sweet and soft.

"Mike!"

"Mmm." His tongue traced an intricate pattern that had her
gripping his hair like a steering wheel.

He guessed she liked that. And so he did it again. And
again. And again.

She bucked, twisting on his sheets, squeezing his head in the
vice-like grip of her thighs.

And he wanted more.

One finger inside. Two.

"*Fuck*, I'm going to—"

She exploded around him, drenching his mouth, holding
him tight both inside and out for a long moment before
collapsing back to the bed.

Mike rode out the wave with her, gentling her descent back
to reality. Only when she had stopped convulsing around him
did he remove his fingers and sit up.

A kiss to that pretty mouth of hers, sipping in her rapid
exhales as she tried to get her breath back. A touch of his lips to
the space between her breasts, to one nipple, the other.

"Mike," she breathed.

He tucked a strand of hair behind her ear. "Like you saying
my name like that."

Her eyes slid closed and a smile smoothed her features. Her
breathing went slow and even.

Sleep. She'd fallen asleep.

Mike almost didn't care. Yes, he was hard and aching,

covered in a layer of sweat, and his balls were probably indigo, but this was Sara.

His Sara.

He tugged a blanket from the bottom of the bed, covered them, and pulled her into his arms.

As she nestled against his chest, her hair got all up in his face. He was so hard that his dick could hammer a fucking nail and she immediately hogged the blanket.

But he didn't give a damn because she was next to him.

FIFTEEN

Sara

SARA WOKE UP WONDERFULLY WARM. She stretched, frowning at the soreness of her muscles, the stiffness of her right hip and ribs.

Had she overdone her run the day before?

But then she registered the heavy arm across her middle, the rough hair of legs pressing against the back of hers, the erection prodding her butt.

And—*shit!* She'd fallen asleep.

She'd had one orgasm and then *fallen asleep*.

Before Mike had gotten his.

Guilt poured over her. She'd basically assaulted him in his closet, begged that he have sex with her, gotten hers . . . and fallen asleep.

Good Lord, she was the *guy*.

That thought made a giggle bubble up in her throat.

But *dang*, she was a jerk. Once he woke up, she needed to find a way to—

"What's so funny?" Mike's voice was raspy from sleep.

She rolled over and stared into his brown eyes. They were soft, not irritated, but there was an underlying heat in them reminding her quite blatantly that she'd left her man hard and unsatisfied the previous night.

Her man?

Had she honestly just thought that?

Except what else was Mike if he wasn't hers?

She'd belonged to him in some way—they'd had this unbreakable, silent connection—since she was sixteen and he was eighteen. Wasn't that the definition of *hers*?

Whatever. She wasn't going to spend time worrying about it. Instead, she was going to embrace it, enjoy it. It had been ages since she'd felt this alive.

Mike made her feel whole.

And since she was embracing this whole *her man* thing, then she was going to take very good care of him.

"Sara?" He touched her cheek. "You okay?"

Her lips curved, and she turned her head so that she could kiss his palm. "I'm better than okay."

One brown brow lifted. "Yeah?"

Sunlight poured through the windows, turning Mike into the equivalent of a Roman god. His skin was golden-hued, his chest squeezable, his abs clearly defined.

She pushed him back against the gray comforter, letting the blanket he must have covered them with slide down her back as she straddled him.

"Six yummy squares," she murmured, running a finger around the defined muscles. "I hear they're hard to get."

Mike hissed out a breath when she moved up and brushed his nipple. "Well, when you don't have anything else to do besides working out . . ."

Mmm. Pecs. They overflowed her hands when she gave them a squeeze. "Really?" she asked and bent down to press a kiss to his chest, then to each of those six squares. "Not anything to *do?*"

She traced her tongue along that little trail of hair that disappeared beneath his boxer briefs, that led to his decidedly *not* little erection, and pushed the waistband down, her mouth actually watering—

And found herself on her back, Mike above her, eyes hot, hard body pressing into her . . . everywhere.

"I believe I promised you multiple orgasms."

"I—"

She didn't get more than that one syllable out before his mouth was on her breasts. The sound that came from her was almost inhuman, but Mike didn't seem to mind, just switched to the neglected side.

He ran a hand down her torso, tracing his fingers straight down and in . . . *in.*

"Mike!" she cried.

"Like it when you call out my name, sweetheart."

Her vision was blurry, her every nerve was on edge, and she was rapidly approaching—

No.

But she was already over the brink, cruising over the peak, cascading down the other side. Pleasure made her limbs lax and her legs—which had been squeezing his arm like a vise—flop open to the mattress.

"What did you put in that ice cream?" she asked, suddenly way too relaxed to move.

He laughed and she joined in, loving the light in his eyes. It felt like those mornings from before. Just the two of them sharing a private joke, her and Mike against the rest of the world. Only *this* time, there weren't barriers—age, parents, responsibilities, *clothes*—between them.

With difficulty, she lifted her arm, which may as well have

been a limp noodle at this point, and touched his cheek.

"I've missed you."

The brown of his eyes intensified as he propped himself up, his elbows on either side of her head. "That's almost better than hearing my name, Jumping Bean."

She stroked the bristles on his jaw, loved the feel of him over her, pressing down, all hard and hot. "We need to talk."

A pained expression crossed his face, but Mike nodded and sat back.

Huh? *Oh!*

"Not now," Sara said, lurching upward to latch onto his shoulder. She flopped down, pulling him along with her. "I meant that as a sometime-later discussion."

"Thank fuck," he said, cupping her face in his palms and leaning down to kiss her.

Hot lips, a searching tongue, teeth nipping at her jaw, her neck. He was a flurry of motion, transforming her languid pleasure of the minute before into a frenzy of need.

His mouth moved to her breasts and, *yes,* she liked that a whole hell of a lot, but when he slid lower, obviously on the trail to south of the border, Sara'd had enough. Look, obviously, she liked oral sex, and Mike was *really* freaking good at it, but she needed him inside her already.

So she used her yoga moves—which made her actually appreciate the torturous exercise for a change—and stopped him by wrapping her legs around his hips.

"S-Sara," he hissed out.

In fairness, she was hissing too. Because her move had brought his cock right *there*.

She could feel the heat of him against her, so close and yet not *in*, and started to shift her pelvis to close that final bit of distance between them.

Mike stopped her, one big hand spanning her waist. "Hold on, sweetheart."

She couldn't hold on, couldn't wait another second, not after waiting ten years.

Her body was on fire, the need coursing through her almost painful.

And so she tilted her hips and brushed against the hard length of him.

"Fuck!" He thrust forward, the tip of him brushing her heat, but just as quickly he was gone.

"Mike, I—"

"Almost, Sara girl, just—"

The crinkle of a wrapper drew her gaze, and she watched as he rolled a condom on. He was back between her thighs, poised at her entrance a second later.

"Yes?" he asked.

"Yes," she replied before he'd even finished the word.

And *thank God* she had because then he was there, filling her, stretching her from the inside out. But it wasn't just physical. Somehow, he was stretching her heart, filling her soul with more than just—

A swivel of his hips pulled her right out of any semi-rational thoughts she had remaining.

She wrapped her legs tight around his waist, clawed at his arms, and held on tight as Mike rode her like a prized stallion.

In and out, in and out, grinding forward, pressing tightly, retreating . . . basically turning her into a writhing, begging puddle of desire.

But the hottest thing was the way he talked to her. The dirty little sentiments whispered in her ear, naughty enough to make her wetter even as her cheeks flushed.

Her moans were loud, her breathing uneven, and when

Mike ordered her to "Come for me. Now," she didn't consider disobeying.

She exploded.

One, two more thrusts, and he was following suit.

Sara had never heard anything hotter than the long, low groan of Mike's orgasm. It drew hers out, pleasure sliding outward from her center to the rest of her limbs, sparks of sensation exploding along her skin.

Holy shit.

Holy fucking shit.

What in the hell was that?

That was soul-shattering, incredible sex, and it meant—

Fuck. What did it mean?

She should—

She needed—

Good God. What *did* she need to do? Run? Jump on top of him for round two? Pretend the whole sexual escapade had been mediocre? That it didn't actually mean anything?

Except he'd heard her verbal orchestra of orgasm—scratch that—*orgasms*. He knew it had been good for her.

Mike must have sensed her panic, because although he had his head buried in her shoulder, rapid exhales puffing against his neck, forearms propping him up and preventing his body from crushing hers, he said, "Later, sweetheart. That talking part doesn't have to come now."

The knot twisting her insides loosened, and he rolled them to the side, shifting to cradle her back against his chest.

"It will all be okay."

She nodded, felt her hair slide against his chest. But it was mostly an empty gesture.

There was no way that things would be okay.

Her life didn't work that way.

SIXTEEN

Mike

MIKE REELED as he held Sara.

He'd just had the most incredible sex of his life, and yet he'd lied to his partner in the process.

This thing between them had the potential to destroy them both.

"Did you feel it?"

Her whispered question undid him.

"Fuck yeah, I felt it, sweetheart." He released her, tugging her shoulder until she faced him. When scared blue eyes met his, he leaned forward and kissed her. He forced his panic to the side, forced that fear of getting burned away, and let himself get lost in the embrace.

This is what he needed to focus on.

Not the what-ifs.

Sara's expression was slightly less petrified when he pulled back. Or at least there was heat and desire tempering her concern.

"We'll figure it out, yeah?"

A nod.

"Together this time." He rested his forehead on hers. "*This* time we're not alone."

She released a breath, and the sweet burst of air caressed his lips. God, he wanted to kiss her again.

He wanted to make love to her again.

But before they could, he needed to know that she was with him.

"Yeah?"

She rolled her eyes. "I've always loved when you don't give me a second to think and push me for an answer."

"I've always loved your sarcasm."

"Yeah?"

He chuckled.

Her shoulders lifted and dropped on a breath. "Okay."

"So we're doing this?"

Sara smiled and sat up. "I thought we were going to talk later."

Mike's breath caught when she slipped from the bed then turned in the direction of the bathroom.

He'd appreciated the up-close view of Sara's body, but seeing her like this: sunshine dappling her skin, her ass jiggling slightly as she strode unabashedly across the bedroom, the little peek-a-boo of side boob as she paused at the door to the bathroom and crooked a finger at him, the red scar along her spine, an angry line leading to her hip—

What?

He was up and out of bed before his eyes had finished processing, standing in the doorway of the bathroom, staring at the mark in horror.

"Shouldn't you deal with that?" Sara pointed at the condom he still wore, bending over to peek in a cabinet, then another, as she searched for something.

On her third try—and he wasn't even in the right frame of mind to appreciate the sight—she pulled out three towels. He still stood on the threshold, but when she tossed a box of tissues at him, he mechanically caught it and took care of the condom.

Sara hung the towels over the side of the shower then opened the glass door and cranked on the water.

Only after she'd adjusted the temperature and turned back around did she seem to realize he hadn't moved.

"What's the matter?"

Fury boiled under his skin, blood actually pounded in his ears. *Thump-thump. Thump-thump. Thump-thump.*

Because he knew what that scar was shaped like.

A skate blade.

Sara's eyes closed, her chest lifted on a long inhale. She let that breath out slowly before speaking. "It's not what you think."

"My mind is not in a good place, Sara. So you'd better explain. Quickly."

She crossed her arms. "Don't be an asshole. I don't *have* to tell you anything. You're not my father or my boss or—"

"I'm the man who was inside you less than five minutes ago."

Twin spots of pink appeared on her cheeks. "That's not the point."

He was across the bathroom in two strides, his chest against hers, pressing her back against the shower wall. Water sluiced over their skin, heated trails dripping down his face, soaking into her hair. He reached an arm behind him and closed the door.

"The point is that I thought we were doing this together."

Her expression was as furious as he felt. "The future. Building something together doesn't mean we need to rehash every fucking thing from our past." She lifted her chin, fixed him with a glare. "Especially shit that doesn't matter."

Except, if it really didn't matter, then she would just tell him.

"Spill it, Sara girl."

"There's nothing to *spill*," she ground out, trying to slip to the side.

Mike pinned her in place with his hips and grabbed her cheeks, forcing her eyes to his when she might have turned her stare away. "Yes. There is."

"No." Her lips pressed flat. "There isn't."

This couldn't work. He didn't have a chance at out-stubborning Sara. Never could.

So Mike changed tactics. He kissed her, hard and hot and enticing, and when he broke away, they were both panting. Sara was no longer trying to escape him; rather, she was leaning into him and rubbing her breasts across his chest.

He liked that. Probably too much since he was trying to be lucid enough to figure out why in the fuck his girl had a ten-inch scar along her back.

Just the thought of that jagged, angry line infuriated him enough to pull blood from his dick and funnel it north to get his brain to work.

"How'd you get the scar?"

Her head plunked back against the tile, slipping her cheeks free of his grasp. "Can't you just let it go?"

He pushed a strand of sodden hair off her face. "No, honey. I'm sorry. I can't."

His tone was gentle, the words soft.

And finally, they seemed to get through her armor.

She swallowed hard. "I'll tell you. But let's shower first. I—I can't do this here."

Mike started to open his mouth, to ask why location made a difference, but Sara raised a hand to his jaw.

"It'll make sense later." Her smile was sad. "Just know I need to be warm and dry to tell it, okay?"

He nodded and stepped back, letting her have most of the water. When she'd wet her hair, he handed her shampoo then soap.

"Sorry," he murmured. "I don't have that conditioner stuff girls use."

Another smile that didn't reach her eyes. "I'll survive."

Unfortunately, Mike thought the sentiment was all too true.

SEVENTEEN

Sara

SARA CLENCHED the towel tightly to her breasts, watching Mike rub the cotton along his chest and legs before tying it around his waist.

Unfortunately, she was completely unable to appreciate the sight.

Why hadn't she realized that he would see the scar?

Of course he would notice.

Impulsivity.

Always her downfall.

"Here."

She blinked. Mike had slipped out of the bathroom and dressed without her noticing. He wore sweats and was holding a shirt out for her.

"Oh," she murmured, fumbling to hold the towel and grab the slip of cotton. Both fell from her fingers, puddled on the floor. "Crap."

"Don't move." He bent, slung the t-shirt over his shoulder,

then picked up the towel. But when he brought the terrycloth around to her back, she flinched away.

Not the scar. Don't touch me there.

"I said don't move." And gently, oh . . . so . . . gently, Mike brushed the towel along her back, up her spine, between her shoulders, mopping up the water she'd missed.

He slipped the shirt over her head and lifted her into his arms. A moment later, she was back in bed, under the covers and cradled against Mike's chest.

The position hurt her hip, and she shifted, feeling her mind clear slightly when his arms came up to hold her in place.

It almost made her smile, almost, when the hard limbs gripped her tighter.

"It happened six years ago," she said, picking up his hand so she could adjust her position, to allow her aching hip some relief. "I really should be more fully recovered. I mean, I can run again, within reason, but yoga is still a pain. Not that I really work at it. It's still Satan's idea of exercise. I'm fine. It's just that things get stiff if I'm in one spot for too long or if I do some new activity—"

She broke off. One, because she was rambling, and, two, because she realized what *new* activity she'd participated in the previous evening. Her cheeks felt red-hot, and her eyes shot to Mike's.

"I like that, sweetheart," he murmured. "That this isn't common for you, that I'm one of the few men who get to touch you—"

"The one man."

He frowned. "What?"

"You're the one man I've been with," she said then hurried to add when his face paled, "Not ever. Just since the accident." Sara shrugged. "It's why I forgot about the scar."

His silence was followed by a long, slow breath. "That's good."

She frowned at the relief in his words. "Would it have mattered if I *was* a virgin?"

Now was his turn to frown. "Is this a trick question?"

"No." Sara tugged at the comforter. The man was like a furnace wrapped around her, an electric blanket on steroids. "But why would you care if I had been one?"

"Why would I care if you'd been a virgin?" he asked, lifting his arm and pulling down the blanket so it was at their waists rather than their shoulders.

She huffed out a breath, stilled his hand when it went to crawl under the hem of her t-shirt. "Yes. Why that?"

"Because I would have wanted to do a better job."

Oh. *Oh.*

And somehow sprawled in bed, bickering with Mike about something completely unimportant was right.

The story, the truth about the accident slipped from her almost as easily as breathing . . . or maybe it was like getting her breath back after the wind had been knocked from her lungs.

Painful but necessary.

"I'd gone on several dates with Leo Tomskoi after the I'd won the gold, but it never went anywhere. We were both too busy—he was on the professional ski circuit, and I had the skating tour, interviews, endorsements, visits to schools. You name it. My agent and publicist had me signed up for it."

"Sounds exhausting."

She smiled. "Yeah. But exhilarating too. You know I always loved that side of it." Her lips twisted. "Especially since the press had been nothing but kind to me."

"You were good at being the media darling." A brush of his fingers across her cheek. "Too charismatic by half."

"Except with you."

"If you only knew." His words were so tortured that Sara started to ask what was wrong, but he waved her off. "Then what happened?"

"He called me a few years after everything came out, said he knew I wouldn't cheat, that he didn't believe a word of the press's nonsense." The parallels between him and Mike were obvious. Except, of course, for the fact that Mike actually believed her. And Leo . . . well, Leo had wanted to get back at her.

A hand slid down her spine, and she shuddered out a breath. "He took me out on one date, then another, then he kidnapped me—"

Sara felt him stiffen beneath her. "Not like that. I mean it was supposed to be romantic, and it was. In a way." She shook her head. Rambling again. "Leo blindfolded me, took me to a frozen pond. He had blankets and food, ice skates and candles."

The moon had been bright on that clear night, the stars cheerfully visible. It had been cold as hell, of course, but the most romantic gesture ever.

Or so she'd thought.

And those skates. *Her* skates. They were her kryptonite.

"Turned out his stepsister was Rebecca Julian. She'd finished third at Nationals." Her words caught in her throat. "I —I didn't even know they were related."

"What happened?" Two words, deadly soft.

Sara remembered the surprise push from behind as Leo had leaned down to kiss her, the crack of her face against the ice when he'd moved back to let her fall, the burn as the cold made contact with her exposed skin. She remembered the blood from her nose dripping down her face as she'd looked up to see Leo skating away.

And then the agony of sharp steel piercing skin.

Rebecca Julian had never made it to the highest level of competition.

Because of Sara.

Because of the cheating.

Because Sara had taken *her* spot.

"I got cut." Rebecca had stepped on her, trampled Sara beneath a skate blade like a toddler crunching a fallen leaf. "They left me out there."

"Sara, honey." Gritted out words, false calm from Mike in the wake of furious brown eyes. "That's not an answer."

"She shoved me down. I was cut by an errant blade, and they left." Sara shuddered, remembering the blood—hot at first, then cold, *so cold*—spreading over her skin.

"They found me the next morning. I had frostbite on my fingers, my nose, but the worst was obviously the injury on my back."

"They left you?" If Mike had been furious before, now that fury looked like mild irritation. "They sliced you with a fucking skate blade and left you to die?"

"I didn't say—"

"You didn't have to!"

He erupted out of bed and paced the room in rage-filled strides. Curse words spewed through the air, many of which she'd thought plenty of times over the years.

"I didn't learn until later that an anonymous male caller had phoned the police that morning. Made sure I didn't die out there."

Leo had an episode of conscience. Or so she presumed.

By the time she'd reached the point of asking, months later in her recovery, he hadn't taken her calls.

Not her finest moment, letting that pass, putting off the doctors and police when they pointed out that her very illogical cutting-herself-on-her-back-with-her-own-skate-blade   explanation was impossible.

But she also couldn't completely regret the act and her passivity.

Her cowardice was why she'd come to San Francisco in the first place. Running.

Sara had wanted to get as far away from her old life as possible. Somewhere warm, somewhere large with a community for artists. She'd wanted to get lost in a big city, but not one rampant with paparazzi.

L.A. had been out.

San Francisco in.

"Fuck!" Mike. She'd been viscerally aware of his agitation, of his pacing and muttered curses, but the outburst still made her jump.

"It's—"

Furious brown eyes whipped toward her. "If you're going to finish that sentence with *okay* then don't bother." He was at the bed in an instant. "You're not close to okay, Sara. You're so far fucked that I don't know how to fix you."

Wow.

She'd always been surprised that words could hurt so badly when they didn't create a mark.

Or a physical one, anyway.

Because that slice across her heart . . .

Her breath whooshed out in a rush. "I've never asked you to fix me."

Sara *should* have said she didn't need fixing, that she was perfect the way she was. But she wasn't delusional.

She had problems.

"Christ." He thrust a hand through his hair. "You never do, Sara. You never do."

"What is that supposed to mean?" She clutched the blankets to her chest, a cotton barrier against whatever he was going to say next.

"It means—" Mike blew out a breath, shook his head.

His phone buzzed.

"It means I've got to get to the airport for the team's flight." He crossed to the closet, words suddenly rushed and brusque. "We're flying to Los Angeles for our game against the Kings. I'll be home late tonight. We'll have to table this until tomorrow."

Table this?

This being the discussion about the story he'd all but forced out of her?

The story that had made him furious . . . at her. Logically, she could understand anger as a reaction to what had happened to her. She'd been angry plenty of times over the last six years, at herself for not going to the police, at Leo and Rebecca for wanting to hurt her. But that didn't make Mike's reaction any more palatable.

She wanted him to be mad for her, not mad *at* her.

"Mike," she said.

He popped his head out. "Do we really have to do this now? I've got stuff to do."

"For the game," she said, expressionless.

"Yes, of course for the game."

And she might have believed him, if not for the look in his eyes.

He wanted her gone.

Well, that problem, at least, she could solve.

After tossing the covers aside, Sara stood and snagged her clothes. She was glad she'd had the foresight to fold and stash them on the armchair in the corner of the room.

It made getting dressed quick work.

Mike was talking again, something about pregame routines and puck drop, flights home and potential delays. She ignored him, slipping into her shoes then opening the app on her phone to call an Uber.

One staircase down with stiff legs, one alarm-code input, one door shut behind her.

The Uber pulled up as she was approaching the gate. She was inside, and it was driving away before the metal barrier had begun to close.

Silence reigned on the way to her apartment.

The driver didn't speak, her phone didn't ring, didn't buzz, and her heart . . . that fragile organ, a delicate papier-mâché project still forming—attempting to dry even as its wet weight tried to collapse in on itself—cracked and crumbled.

It dissolved to ash.

But ash sometimes made the strongest type of armor.

EIGHTEEN

Mike

MIKE SHOULD HAVE FELT like the biggest jackass on the planet when he walked, fully dressed, out of the closet and found his bedroom empty.

But he didn't.

Hence, the Biggest Jackass Award.

Instead, the emotion that poured through him was relief.

Relief that he didn't need to hash out the feelings inside him, that he didn't need to face the guilt.

Yes. Guilt.

Why had he let Sara go?

Everything was his fault.

"Fuck," he muttered and swiped a hand down his face.

The martyr complex was stupid, he understood that. He knew it was impossible to control the rest of the world, that he wouldn't have been able to stop her coaches from cheating her, couldn't have hoped to prevent the betrayal.

But he would have been there for her.

She wouldn't have been alone.

"Fuck," he said again and strode from the room. It still smelled like Sara, soft and floral and with just the barest hint of pencil lead. The scent may as well have been embedded into his pores.

He pounded down the stairs, twisted the knob for the door leading to the garage, and stopped.

Had that been there the night before? Or had Sara dropped—

Shaking his head, Mike picked up the folded piece of paper. Of course it hadn't been in the middle of the floor last night. It was obviously one of Sara's drawings, the material the thick white paper from her sketchbooks.

He opened it.

Then almost wished he hadn't.

The drawing was of him and Sara, their faces young, their expressions carefree. The background was the part that gutted him. Slashes and swirls, pencil strokes that were harsh and painful.

Hidden in those writhing lines were older versions of him and Sara. Her face was long and gaunt, tears pouring like blood from her eyes, and he stood, brows pulled tight into a frown, eyes dark and disapproving.

Her tears swirled between the two of them, dripped down to surround their younger selves. It didn't quite reach them, those youthful masks untouched.

But it was what was beneath it all that caused the greatest pain.

She'd done the whole piece in shades of gray, and Mike couldn't help but think that was how she viewed the world.

Lacking in color.

Pain locked beneath cheerful facades.

And suddenly the guilt that had been harping on him a bare half hour before felt like peaches and rainbows. Because *this* guilt—the turning on her when she'd trusted him enough to open up—was a thousand times worse.

He'd hurt her.

Mike cursed for what felt like the hundredth time that hour.

He slammed into the garage, whipping his phone from his pocket and pressing the opener. It rattled up as he dialed and shoved himself into his car.

Stefan answered, sounding suitably distracted.

Mike was sure Brit had something to do with that, especially when he heard a feminine giggle in the background.

Gross.

But the nauseous feeling that was making his gut churn wasn't the thought of his teammates doing a horizontal line change.

He'd hurt Sara. Again.

Jackass of the year. Fuck. The century.

He waited impatiently for the gate to open and sped down the road, back into the city, and away from the airport.

Hence the phone call.

Stefan's voice sharpened, the giggle cut off. "Mike? You okay?"

"No." He swerved around the corner, zipped onto 101 and went north. "I fucked up. Big time."

"Was it the charm? I really thought you could pull some out of—"

"Not the charm," he ground out, pushing his speed. He'd done well with the charm. Scavenger hunt with all her favorite things. Check. Flowers. Check. Multiple orgasms. Check, check, check.

The problem was his stunted little man-child emotions.

"Then what, buddy? 'Cause I thought you'd decided to go for it. I talked to the team's publicist—"

"What?" Mike almost rear-ended the car in front of him.

"Not in specifics," Stefan rushed to say. "I never mentioned her name or even alluded to Sara's troubles. I just asked her to think of some ways to spin a relationship with a player and a person who might be considered infamous—wrongly, of course," he added when Mike spat out a curse.

He didn't like the idea of airing Sara's dirty laundry but hated more that *he* hadn't thought of working with the powers that be preemptively.

If he wanted to protect Sara, then he needed to think of these things first, not rely on his teammates to bail them out.

But that wasn't important because—

"Her story got worse."

"How could it possibly be worse?"

Mike cut over two lanes and took the exit that would lead to Sara's apartment. "Trust me. It did."

"Fuck," Stefan said. "I'm assuming you can't tell me the specifics."

Mike paused at a signal. "Not my story to tell."

"Yeah. Figured." A sigh that slid through the airwaves. "So what now? It's not your fault that her life got worse."

"It is when you're so pissed and angry at the people that hurt her that you don't realize she needed a freaking hug."

Or kind words. Or reaffirmation that it hadn't been her fault.

The light turned green, and he smashed down the accelerator.

"You need to grovel."

"That much is clear," he snapped. "But I have to find her first."

"She left? Fuck, man. You really did screw up."

"Yeah. Sara's got a habit of running when things go bad, and I—"

He hadn't helped matters. He'd freaked, and now she thought he was blaming her and—

"So what do you need me to do?"

The signal turned red, and Mike screeched the car to a stop. Right ahead. Then another left, and he'd be at her apartment.

"Just cover for me with Bernard if I'm late. I should be good but . . ." He trailed off, not really knowing if he'd be good at all. Not if he didn't find Sara and convince her to forgive him.

But his mind was in a fucked-up air space. If he didn't at least try . . .

"Will do." Stefan paused. "It'll be okay."

"How do you know that?" Mike screeched to a halt on the street in front of Sara's apartment.

"Because I'm guessing that Sara already knows you're an idiot."

"I'm hanging up now, asshole."

"I got one more tidbit bit of advice for you, buddy."

"You can take your advice and stick it straight up—"

Stefan didn't let him finish. "In all seriousness, know that I'm—"

A muffled female voice said something.

"—correction, *we're* here for you."

"Thanks. I think."

"Oh, and Mike?"

He popped the door, hesitated before opening it to get out. "Yeah."

"Groveling works better when you get down on both knees."

NINETEEN

Sara

WHY DID SHE *ALWAYS* RUN?

It was pathetic, really, how quickly she cut her losses and took off. What was even more pathetic was the fact that she was tying her sneakers and getting ready to take an actual run, rather than the Uber one from Mike's place.

Her hip didn't need the extra pounding—

And, great, now she was blushing because her mind couldn't think of the word *pounding* without conjuring images of Mike and how good it had felt when he'd pounded into her.

Hot skin, hard muscles—

Sharp words.

Cowardice.

"Goddammit," she muttered and wrestled her hair into a ponytail.

She'd run. Left without standing up for herself.

Maybe she and Mike wouldn't work out. Maybe they couldn't get over all the shared and individual baggage they carried.

But she hadn't fought. For any of it.

Instead, she'd rolled over and died. Again.

Pathetic. And yup, her picture was going in that proverbial dictionary. Sara Jetty: cheating ice princess and connoisseur of avoiding any and all conflict.

Shoving in her earbuds with one hand, she twisted the knob with the other.

The door pushed open, almost smacking her in the face.

In fact, it *would* have smacked her had a large, strong hand not caught the plank of wood and stopped it a half inch from her nose.

She knew those hands. Knew that scar across the ring finger, knew the light dusting of hair on the knuckles.

Slowly, the door was drawn back, and Mike slipped inside her apartment.

He raised a brow at her, no doubt taking in her sweats, sneakers, and firmly contained ponytail. "Going somewhere?"

She lifted her chin, tried to pretend that her heart wasn't racing.

Why was he here? Why did she care so damn much?

"Yeah. For a run."

"Seems to be a lot of that happening."

Her arms crossed on their own, she'd swear it. Either that or Mike had the uncanny ability to piss her off faster than any other person on the planet. "Not really."

"Yeah?" He closed the door behind him, leaned back against it. "So you're going to tell me you didn't run from my house?"

Sara ripped her earbuds out and walked over to her small sitting area. The armchair was a soft blue velvet and beyond worn, but it was the perfect height for her little round table that played double duty as both work space and kitchen counter.

She slammed her phone down onto the table, not caring when the cord to her headphones tangled and the little plastic speakers collided with her cup of pencils, almost knocking it over.

Her mad was on and raring now, and it felt *so* much better than the hurt from before.

Leaving the phone, she whirled around and marched over to Mike. Poked him in the chest. "Don't try and tell me for one second that you didn't want me gone. You all but ripped the truth from me then wanted me to GTFO."

He propped one foot behind him on the door.

It should have irritated her, that action. He was getting street scum on her walls, probably marking up the paint. And yet her mind literally would not let her focus on anything aside from the fact that he could fill out those slacks.

Really fill them out.

As in, she knew now from personal experience how well he could fill out a pair of pants.

Whew.

Was it getting hot in her apartment?

She pulled at the collar of her shirt, needing some cool air on her heated skin.

"I don't know what that means."

"What *what* means?"

Mike snagged her wrist, pressed her palm to his chest. He wore a suit jacket and button-down, so there were at least two layers between her hand and his skin, but her body didn't know the difference.

Or hell, maybe it did.

Because her lady parts were demanding that she slip those buttons loose, part the shirt, and lick his pecs like a popsicle.

"I don't know what G T F O means."

"Get the fuck out."

He blinked, dropped his fingers from her wrist.

The action was abrupt enough for her undressing fantasy to

waver, enough for her to realize it was just that. A fantasy.

She and Mike were only a fantasy.

"I—" He cocked his head, eyes flashing to the ceiling as he worked something out in his brain. "Oh. *Oh.*"

"What?"

"GTFO means to get the fuck out."

Well, yeah.

"Not that you want me to leave now."

Except, now that he mentioned it . . .

He flashed her a grin. "Tell me how you really feel, Sara girl."

She huffed. "I *thought* I just did." Turning, she sighed again. "Mike. You wanted me gone. You don't like what happened to me. I get that. But—" Her chair creaked as she sank down into it and dropped her head into her hands. "Truth is, you wanted me to leave."

"Yes."

All traces of heat vanished, her body iced over. "Why don't *you* tell me how you really feel?"

That had come out on a steady voice. If nothing else, there was that. Her hurt was hidden so deep that no one would ever know.

Except for Mike.

Because the jerkwad always saw beneath her armor.

This time was no exception.

He cursed and was in front of her in a second, hands on her knees, face between her arms, forcing her to look at him.

"Sweetheart."

Sara leaned back, crossed her arms. "Don't call me that."

Mike's lips twitched. "Fine. Sara girl, I'm not mad at you. I'm mad at myself."

"Well, I'm pissed as hell at *you.*"

The twitch transformed into a full-blown grin. "God, I like

you." Her heart stuttered, her words caught in her throat. He stroked a finger down her cheek. "Nothing to say about that one?"

How could she?

He'd taken her armor—the one made from the ashes of her heart—and crumbled it effortlessly under the slightest show of charm.

At her silence, he sobered. "I should have been there to protect you."

She found her voice . . . or at least her scoff. "Protect me from whom?"

"I—"

"My coaches? The media? No one could have protected me from that circus."

His phone buzzed, and he pulled it from his pocket with a curse.

"None of this is your fault." She shook her head. "I should have realized what was going on long before it all came out. I knew—"

Eyes flashed up to hers. "Knew what?"

"That something was off during the competition." She sighed. "I thought it was nerves—"

"Except you never got nervous."

No. She hadn't.

"Born and bred for skating competitions" was what her coaches had always said.

"Clutch," her brother had called it.

Her mother had referred to it as *"grace under pressure."*

But that time it had been different. She'd thought it the large scale, the high stakes, the pressure.

How wrong she'd been.

"Anyway, you need to go," she said, standing and forcing him to back up. "The team's got to be leaving soon."

"I—"

She turned and walked toward the door. "Your team needs you."

"*You* need me."

Armor was a joke. She had none when it came to Mike. "Come here," she said.

"What?"

"Just come here."

He rose to his feet and crossed to her. When he was within arm's reach, she launched herself at him. He caught her—as she'd known he would—and pulled her tight against his chest.

"Thank you for coming after me."

"I may have been an idiot back then, but I'm not one now."

She snorted.

"Okay, I'm still an idiot, just slightly smaller in magnitude. How's that?"

"Reasonable."

His breath ruffled her ponytail as he chuckled. Sara rubbed her cheek against the crisp cotton of his button down. He smelled . . . like him. "I'll always come for you," he said, "so no more running, okay?"

"Again reasonable."

Arms loosening, he smiled down at her. "We're both going to give this our best chance, yes?" he asked, and when she nodded, pressed his lips to hers softly.

Before the pleasant fire, the stoked flames could turn into a full-raging inferno, Sara stepped back.

She raised a fist. "Do our best."

Mike's eyes went wide at the gesture. They'd said it each time before going their separate ways in the rink. A fist bump and—

"Do our best," he murmured, tapping his much larger hand against hers.

TWENTY

Mike

MIKE MADE it to the plane with literally minutes to spare.

Which meant that the only open seat was next to Max and his collection of plastic toys—sorry, *figurines*.

"It's a short flight," he muttered under his breath as he walked down the aisle and stowed his bag.

One hour. He could make it through one hour.

"How's it?" Max asked, pulling out a *Walking Dead* graphic novel instead of a bucket of toys.

Thank fuck.

"Fine." He plugged in his headphones and . . . waited.

"What did you think of last week's episode?"

Mike knew he had two choices: either answer the question and hope Max got on a monologue about some minuscule detail of the show, or draw out the torture and ignore him.

In which case, Max's questions would just continue until he wore Mike down and he answered anyway.

So Mike asked, "What show?"

"*Walking Dead,* of course."

"I don't watch zombie shows."

"What about zombie movies?"

He shrugged. "Nope. I'm not into the whole post-apocalyptic thing."

"*What?* How can you not like Mila Jochavick in the *Resident Evil* franchise? She's hot and kickass and . . ."

And there he went. Mike turned on his music, Max's droning about zombies becoming pleasant background noise.

"Do you have a minute?" Mike asked Bernard.

Their head coach paused the video he was watching on his iPad before glancing up. "Come in."

Mike stepped to the side, letting Stefan walk into the office Coach had commandeered first. Then he shut the door and sat down.

Bushy white brows were drawn together. "Want to tell me what this is about?"

"Stefan knows some of the story, but I thought as captain, he should know the rest." Mike shrugged. "And I didn't want you to be out of the loop when this all comes out."

Bernard set his iPad aside. He didn't ask the question, that wasn't his way, but instead waited for Mike to give him the remainder of the story.

"I grew up with Sara Jetty."

Stefan's breath hissed out, Coach didn't react so obviously. Instead, he leaned back in his chair and pressed his palms to his desk.

"We skated at the same rink for years, I drove us both to practices before school, ate dinner at her family's house more often than my own." Mike paused as those memories ran wild in his mind.

Sara sweet and soft and shy.

Sara on the cusp of being a woman.

Sara strong and competitive and hardworking.

"And?" Coach prompted.

"I was in love with her then, but she left for the to win herself a gold medal, and I left for juniors and—" He stopped, not wanting to share his reasons for staying away. Not when Stefan and Coach didn't need to know.

"You grew apart?" Stefan asked.

A nod. "We were young, busy with our own stuff, but then I ran into her in the city a few weeks ago. She's working as an artist, and things are . . . well, like they were before." He straightened his shoulders. "We've decided to give us as a couple a try. I wanted you to know only because of the potential blowback on the team."

Coach pressed his lips together.

"I know no one gives a shit about me, but Sara's past—" A shrug. "I don't want to screw with the team, not when we're playing so well, but at the same time . . ."

Sara was important.

More important than anything else.

"I'll discuss with upper management. Stefan, you'll deal with anything that comes up on the team side. Come to me only if you have to. I don't want to be the host of a fucking dating show."

Nice.

"But that being said"—Bernard leaned forward in his chair —"I'm proud of you, son. Proud that you got your shit together last season and proud that you're thinking of the team enough to come to me with this."

The words hit him straight in the gut.

Or hell, if he was getting sappy, right in the heart.

Which was an organ he'd thought totally decimated. But

between Sara and Coach going all Hallmark-moment and his girl-talk with Stefan, the little blood-pumper was making a comeback.

Bernard picked up his iPad, dismissing them as effectively as his words. "Why are you still here?"

They bolted, closing the door behind them.

"So you worked things out?" Stefan asked as they walked to the visitors' locker room.

"Yeah." Mike sighed. "Or as much as I could before I had to go. She's at least willing to give me a shot."

"That's something." Stefan stopped outside the locker room entrance. "I hesitate to suggest this, given what happened after I told you to use your charm, but you've got to woo her, bud. Show her how good it could be between you two. Help her understand that the notoriety she's risking dating you will be worth it, 'cuz you're so awesome."

"Woo her? What is this, 1840?"

"No. If it was, you'd have compromised her and already be married." He put his hands up when Mike just stared at him, mouth agape. "Look, I may have read a few of Brit's historical romance books."

Mike chortled then didn't—couldn't—hold back. He burst out laughing. "Whipped, man. You're so fucking whipped."

"Hey, I'm also the one getting sex every night, so suck on that."

"No, thanks. You're not my type."

Stefan huffed. "I liked it better when you were a surly S.O.B. who didn't talk."

"No, you didn't."

"Fine," Stefan said. "Forget about the wooing, just don't fuck it up. How about that?"

Mike sobered, straightened, and tapped his captain on the shoulder. "*That* is pretty much the best advice I've ever gotten."

Shaking his head, Stefan turned and walked into the locker room. "You're insane, Stewart. Totally certifiable."

Mike followed him, and later, after the game was over and he was slipping back into his suit, he noticed something poking out of the corner of his messenger bag.

Fucking Max. Probably one of those goddamned graphic novels he was spouting about on the plane. It wouldn't have been the first time that he'd tried to convert Mike over to the fine religion of nerdom.

Except it wasn't a graphic novel.

Or, at least, not the type that Max read.

On this book's cover were a man and woman. The man was shirtless, and he held the woman, who was wearing a huge, bright-purple dress—that conveniently appeared to be falling off —close to his chest.

The title talked about seducing a viscount, whatever that was.

A foot nudged his shoe. A feminine foot.

"For inspiration," Brit murmured. "Make sure you read Chapter Twenty."

And with that gem of advice, she walked away.

TWENTY-ONE

Sara

MOONLIGHT AND CLEAR SKIES. The lake called to her, and Sara sketched furiously to capture the image in front of her, to order it with the snapshots in her mind and create art on the paper.

Her hand cramped, the one damaged by frostbite all those years before, and she set her pencil down for a second to stretch it.

Then her hip, which was apparently aching too. And now that her body was on full revolt, her back joined the party.

The muscle spasms took her breath away.

Her bubble—the one that had ensconced her in just the paper and pencil and scene before her eyes—burst. She descended back into reality.

From the outside, it surely looked as though she'd been merely taking a break, stretching those stiff limbs. But on the inside, her mind came down to Earth kicking and screaming.

It wanted to stay lost in her drawing, to be swept along with the softly moving water, to understand its place in a strictly black and white world.

She snorted at her inner idiocy and lay carefully back, trying to get those contracting muscles to relax.

Sara wasn't one of those eccentric artist types; she understood the real world.

She sometimes just didn't want to interact with it.

Her phone buzzed, pulling her fully out of her artist's fog—mental, not literal. It took a moment—those stiff fingers again—to tug it out of her pocket.

Mike.

She smiled and her stomach went all gooey. She swiped. "Hey there, Hot Shot."

"Where the fuck have you been?"

The angry words shocked her and as such, it took her a moment to gather her words.

In the meantime, Mike was having a conversation with himself. "Shit. I didn't mean to sound like that. I've just been worried. I called when we landed, and you didn't answer. And then I went to your apartment, and you didn't respond to the knock. I uh . . . *went* in, and you weren't there—"

"You broke into my apartment?"

"I didn't *break* anything."

"Oh. So you just entered my apartment without a key?"

"You need a better lock." He sounded like such a little petulant child that Sara had to smile.

"Mike."

His sigh rattled through the speaker of her phone. "I was worried."

"I'm sorry," she said, feeling a little bad that she'd scared him, but also touched that he so obviously cared.

It had been a long time since anyone had bothered to worry about her whereabouts.

"Where are you?"

She sat up and tucked her things into her backpack. "Drawing."

"Where?"

"At the Palace of Fine Arts. I'm done now though. Want me to come over?"

"I'll be there in five minutes." A clicking sound, the beep of a horn, and she had to wonder if he was single-handedly screwing with the traffic patterns of San Francisco again.

"Want me to let you drive?"

A pause, then, "I love your voice, Sara."

The L-word made her breath catch. "Oh?"

"Talk to me, sweetheart. What are you working on?"

She slipped her arms into the straps of her backpack. "The lake again. Except this time, no one interrupted my light."

One more glance at the space she'd been working in. Other than a few pencil shavings, which she pushed into the planter bed with her foot, there wasn't any sign of her having been there at all.

Just the way she liked it.

Mike's chuckle drew her focus back to the phone.

"Have I apologized for that?"

"No."

Another chuckle.

Another flutter in her stomach.

"Well, I'm sorry I ruined your light." She heard the clicking sound again, and he said, "I'm turning into the lot now."

"I'm almost there too."

And then she was on the sidewalk, and his car was pulling up next to her. She reached for the handle to let herself in . . . and heard it lock.

Her fingers tried it anyway. No. He'd really locked the door.

The car turned off. Mike slid from the driver's seat with a sexy smile. "Hey."

Three letters and she was mush.

He crossed in front of the hood, paused facing her. "I missed you."

She *pished*. "You just saw me."

"Too long," he said and tugged her into his arms.

Being there was perfect. The embrace, her chest pressed against his, Mike's warmth wrapped around her. "I missed you too."

His laughter puffed by her ear. "Come on. Let's get you home."

Releasing her, he stepped back and pressed the key fob. The passenger door unlocked with a beep.

He pulled the handle, helped her into the seat, and then took her breath away when he reached across her body to turn on the seat warmer.

"Missed you," he murmured again, cupping her jaw for the slightest moment. His eyes were hot and liquid beneath the interior lights. His mouth was right . . . there.

Sara wanted him to kiss her. No. She *needed* his lips across hers, his tongue in her mouth, his cock—

But then he was closing her door and walking around the front of the car. Her heart raced, the space between her thighs ached, and she shifted uncomfortably in her seat.

Especially when Mike rested his hand on her leg, just inches from where she was desperate for it.

Sweat beaded on the back her neck.

She definitely did not need the seat warmer. Reaching forward to turn off the little dial, her eyes happened to flick over to Mike.

Or more specifically, Mike's lap.

He didn't need to be warmed up either, apparently.

A giggle snuck out of her.

Brown eyes flashed over. "What?"

"Nothing."

He'd put the car into drive, but at her rebuff, he clicked it into park again and turned to face her.

In the smallest movement, he'd managed to surround her, one hand on the dash, the other on the back of her seat. "What?" he asked again.

"You're frustrating. You know that?"

He smirked, raised a brow.

"Fine. I was just thinking that I didn't need the seat warmer because you've gotten me so hot."

"Fuck, Sara girl. You can't say things like that here." He nodded at the street in the distance, where even though it was the middle of the night, cars still regularly drove by. "Not when I can't do anything about it."

"Not my fault." She put her hand on his thigh, brushed her fingers against the tip of his erection. He cursed again, and now it was her turn to smirk. "You did ask."

"Sweet Christ, woman. I think you're going to be the death of me."

She started to laugh, but then his mouth was against hers, his tongue slipping in between her parted lips to intertwine with hers. He moved, there was a *click*, and suddenly she was in his lap, pressed between the hardness of his body and the unyielding steering wheel.

His hands were on her breasts, her hips, between her thighs, ramping her up and turning that need from before into frenzied desire.

He pressed his palm firmly against her clit. "Mike!" She bucked—

Honk!

They both jumped and . . .

"Ow!" she moaned as their heads clonked together.

"Sorry," he muttered, one hand on his temple, the other steadying her on his lap.

"You did warn me"—her mouth twitched—"that this wasn't the place."

"Exactly." He set her back in her seat then reached across and re-buckled her seatbelt. "But dang, sweetheart, do we have some chemistry."

She couldn't hold back her grin. "That we do. Now take me home so we can explore it."

TWENTY-TWO

Mike

MIKE DROVE Sara back to her apartment, and despite all of the talk of exploring their *chemistry*, he walked her to her door, waited until she'd opened the lock, and then pulled her into his arms.

The kiss he gave her wasn't the one he wanted, but it was the one she deserved.

Sweet and soft, tender lips and slow strokes, and when, finally, he managed to wrestle himself away, he cupped her cheek.

"Good night, Jumping Bean."

Her brows pulled together into a frown that was both comical and wonderfully cute.

"Night?"

He tugged her bag from her shoulders—the cursed woman had insisted on carrying it herself—and pushed her gently across the threshold into her apartment.

"I have two days off," he said. "Lunch tomorrow?" He glanced out the little window in her living room. The sky was already lightening, and it was nearly dawn. "Or rather, today?"

He'd landed after midnight then spent two of the longest hours of his life worried as hell for Sara.

"But—"

"Oh. Let me see your phone." He plucked it from her back pocket. "What's the code to unlock it?"

Her head was moving from side-to-side, a partial shake, confusion marring her brow.

"What's the code, Sara girl?"

"11-14"

His breath hitched and a long, slow grin curved his mouth. "Really?"

"So what?" she snapped, abruptly defensive. "It doesn't mean anything."

Except it did.

"Yeah?" He pulled his phone from his pocket. "Guess what my code is?"

Blue eyes flew up, collided with his. "Really?"

Mike put the code in on his phone, showed her when it unlocked. "Really."

"Oh."

The numbers were their respective birthdays. "You were on my mind a lot."

Sara swallowed then wrapped her arms around his waist. "You too."

"Okay," he said, when she pulled back. "I'm not going to comment on the late-night exploits and you being too distracted to take your own safety seriously." He stopped, fixed her with a glare. "At some point, we will discuss that."

Her chin lifted for a moment, but then she sighed. "I want to argue with you when you're being all dictatorial. Unfortunately, in this, you're probably right."

"No *probably* about it."

Her mouth opened, and he touched his thumb to her lower lip.

"Let's argue about it later. For now, I want to download the *Find My Friends* app to your phone. So I can see where you are if you're distracted, not to keep tabs," he rushed to add. "You can put it on my phone too. It's not some crazy abusive boyfriend thing, just the easiest solution—"

Soft fingers grabbed her phone from his hand. In a moment, she had the app store open, and it was downloading. "Now you."

He did the same, and they each took a few minutes to get their accounts set up and synced. Seeing their dots next to each other on the home screen felt right.

"Until later, Jumping Bean." Mike pressed a soft kiss to her lips, restrained himself like a grown-ass man so it didn't turn into something way more heated, then started for the stairs.

"I need more nicknames for you, Hot Shot," she said. "The single one I've got can't compete."

He laughed and paused on the top step. "You can call me anything you want." A raised brow. "Or God. That works too."

Her reply was tart, and he loved her all the more for it. "Or Jackass, yeah? That always works well."

"True." He pointed to her apartment. "Now close and lock that door, honey."

She sighed, probably at the endearment. But he couldn't help it. Every sentence that came out of his mouth seemed to need to show her exactly how much she meant to him. Especially since it was way too soon to say the three most important words in his vocabulary.

And contrary to popular belief, those three words were *not* shit, mother, and fucker.

Though those were definitely his second favorite set.

"Night, Mike." He watched the door shut, the deadbolt slide home.

"Night, Sara girl."

———

Whoever had come up with the concept of wooing was a giant asshole.

Mike had Sara exactly where he wanted her. They'd both slept late, and he'd called her mid-afternoon to take her to a late lunch on the waterfront.

Since it was crab season, they'd had their choice of the freshly cooked crustacean before picking up a loaf of sourdough from Boudin's and walking down the backside of Pier 39.

The sea lions were in full force, barking and flopping around on the floating platforms as kids looked on laughing.

They'd found a relatively quiet corner to eat their lunch before heading back to his place to sack out and binge on *Game of Thrones*.

She'd never seen it, and he was tired of Max bugging him about the *"best-show-in-the-history-of-all-shows,"* so they took the plunge together.

Three episodes and they were still going strong.

What was also going strong was his erection.

That particular part of his anatomy could rival those granite statues in Italy.

Sara was curled up against his chest in the media room, cuddled close even though his couch was huge. Not that he minded, except that he'd read the book from Brit on the flight back to the city, finished it after he'd returned home the previous night.

And falling into bed too soon had been the theme of Chapter Twenty.

The main scene in which Brit had underlined repeatedly, writing a giant *No!* in the margin of one page and *Romance!* in the other.

Both of which he'd screwed the pooch on.

Game of Thrones wasn't particularly romantic, now was it? And the sex part . . . Shit, he'd fucked—literally—that up as well.

Though the sea lions had been a nice touch, he thought.

"What's wrong with you?"

Mike blinked. "What?"

"You're all stiff and formal." She popped him on the chest. "When a girl is lying here, she likes to be held. Yes?"

He hadn't even realized that his hands were at his sides instead of around her. He quickly remedied that. "I'm sorry, I just—"

And he shut up because what was he going to say? He'd read a *romance* novel to try and win her over?

Yeah, not happening.

Sara shifted so she was straddling his lap. The television backlit her body, highlighting the blond of her hair, the pale ivory of her skin.

She was so fucking beautiful.

"What's going through that head of yours?" she asked, soft, but there was a layer of steel beneath the words.

No way would she let this go without a straight answer.

And didn't she deserve that much?

"You are the most beautiful thing I have ever seen." Her lips parted, breath hiccupping as it slid through. "I want to do this right, and I'm fucking it all up."

"Okay, overthinker," she said, "I thought we agreed to give this our best shot. So tell me how you're fucking it up. The romantic walk by the bay? The ice cream and sketchpad? The way you've held my hand, touched my back, stroked my cheek?" She smiled and pressed a kiss to his mouth. "You've been romancing me, and I appreciate it. I *love* it." Her brows pulled down. "What I don't appreciate, however, is you being more in your mind than with me."

She held his gaze, and in that moment, he was speechless. Frozen. Because of what was in her eyes.

Warmth. Affection. Desire. Fire.

God, he loved this woman.

Her hands dropped to his shoulders and she leaned in. "I'm not letting you off the hook in the romance department." Her giggle teased his lips. "I want more ice cream, please. But let's just enjoy this moment when it's only us."

Before the outside world intruded.

Because it would, Mike knew that.

"Okay," he murmured and closed the last inch between their mouths.

Heat . . . but more. Love fueled the desire, made it flame with an intensity that should have scared him.

Instead, like a pyromaniac, he embraced the inferno, let it carry him under, and not until he felt the last vestiges of his self-control slipping did he pull back.

He turned Sara on his lap, pulled her back tight against his chest, and looped his arms around her middle.

"But—I—" Her protest was more moan than words. She turned her head toward his, mouth seeking—

"Doing this right, Sara girl." He put a finger to her cheek and gently pressed her face toward the TV screen.

"How about you do *me* instead?"

She squirmed on his lap and, *fuck*, did the motion of her hips against his cock feel incredible.

His hands clamped down on her waist to stay her motion. "Soon, sweetheart. But we're going to take our time."

He didn't want to rush. Not again.

"I don't want time." She rolled her ass against his erection, made stars flash behind his eyes. "I want you inside me."

And every bit of blood left his brain.

It headed south, directly to the part of his body thinking it was an exceptional idea to fuck Sara right there on the couch.

His cell ringing saved him.

That was, until he answered it and realized who was on the other end.

TWENTY-THREE

Sara

MIKE'S entire body changed the moment he heard the person on the other end of the call.

He stiffened, and it wasn't like the formal distance from earlier. His mind wasn't holding him back from connecting with her. *This* reaction was rock-hard, instant fury.

But his hands were gentle.

Head tilting to press the phone between his ear and shoulder, he clasped her waist and carefully slid her to the side.

The couch had been incredibly comfortable, a soft micro-velvet in a cool shade of gray, but now she might as well have been sitting on concrete.

Because something was wrong.

Very, very wrong.

Mike stood and paced the room. Not saying anything as he listened to whoever was speaking, and the longer the call went on, the tenser he became. Rage radiated off his body, spreading into the space around them.

"If you do this—"

Ice cold. His words were a dagger, a frosty sword that should have wounded.

"*No*," he snapped. "It's my turn to talk now. If you do this, if you continue along this path, know we are done." A pause. "Everything. The house. The cars. The art. All gone—"

He stopped for a second as the person he was talking to seemed to cut him off, but only for a second.

"I'm hanging up now. No. I'm. Hanging. Up. Make your choice, and I hope to fucking God that it's the right one."

Sara jumped when the phone clattered down onto the table by her feet.

"What's wrong?"

Mike sat next to her, picked up her hand, and said, "We're out of time, Sara girl. You've got to decide now if we're really doing this."

Her brows pulled down. "I thought we already made that choice."

"Between us, yes." He sighed, shoved his free hand through his hair. "But the rest of the world is about to know. You good with that?"

Flashes.

Burly men screaming her name.

Crowds on the sidewalk yelling obscenities.

Not being able to leave her house, to turn on the TV, to go online.

The images collided with her mind, fear swelled up in her throat, choked off any reply she might have hoped to make.

"I'm sorry, sweetheart." He shook his head. "This isn't how I wanted—"

"Who?"

"What?"

"No. *Who* was on the phone?"

He closed his eyes for a beat before opening them. Regret was clear in their depths. "My mother."

Sara struggled to align the call with what she knew of Mike's mother. But she hardly *knew* anything. Mrs. Stewart had never come to Mike's games, and he'd always hung out at Sara's house, never the other way around.

"She apparently had come into the city to surprise me. Read that as code for hitting me up for money. Again." He stood, fingers slipping from hers as he began to pace the room. "Ostensibly, she saw you come out of my house and decided to follow you. She has pictures of us in my car."

Her brain hurt. Putting aside that his mother had followed her, why the pictures? What had she hoped to accomplish? "I—I guess I don't really understand."

"My mom considers herself an artist." His head dropped back, eyes on the ceiling as he rubbed the back of his neck. "Fuck me. She used to be a pretty damned good one. When she could actually complete a project, that is."

Sara rose to her feet, crossed over to him, and grasped his forearms. "You've got to start at the beginning. I'm . . . well, I'm confused."

"Shit. I'm sorry." He tilted his chin down, met her gaze. "You remember my dad was in that accident and went on permanent disability?"

She nodded. His dad had worked at the local paper mill until a piece of machinery had fallen on his leg and shattered the bones so horribly it had to be amputated below the knee.

"I remember."

"Well, everyone was great about it, getting me to practices, donating money, supporting us until we got back on our feet," he said. "It even gave my mom the opportunity to sell some of her photos. Started her on her career—or what should have been one."

Her fingers tightened unconsciously. "What happened?"

"She hurt her knee pretty bad when she was out shooting one day. Slipped on some ice and just went down hard. There was no way we could afford another doctor's visit, not since we were just getting by."

His hands were fists, his forearms steel beneath her palms. "It's okay—"

"No, it's really not." He laughed, harsh and bitter. "But I know what you're trying to say. Thing is, Jumping Bean, you need to know all of it."

Sara inhaled, released it slowly. "Okay."

"My mom took her first pill that day. My dad was in pain all the time, had a permanent prescription for them, in fact. He wouldn't miss one."

"Or more."

Mike nodded. "A lot more. One turned into a half dozen, which morphed into more than my dad was taking per day. And like a true addict, she hid her addiction until the problem was too large to keep under wraps."

"But how'd she get the pills? Didn't your dad need them?"

"Yup. Except, when you're a patient with as many health problems as my dad, turns out it's easier to up your dosage, to even get another prescription for a different opioid." His shoulders slumped. "My mom learned every trick. Different doctors. Different pharmacies. She had power of attorney for my father, and since part of the settlement with the mill was covering his medical bills, it didn't cost anything. It was almost too easy."

"Why am I sensing the *but* coming?"

He snorted. "Because there is one. While my mom was out on her nature hikes, high out of her mind and definitely not taking pictures, the bills piled up. She wasn't working, wasn't selling her art. We were sinking, only no one knew it."

Pieces began aligning in Sara's mind. Her heart pounded,

her knees trembled. "When, Mike?" she asked, voice shaking. "When did you find out?"

"Two days before you left for Europe." He cursed. "So there it is. My whole sordid tale."

"That's why you—"

Another curse. "I couldn't put that on you. Not then."

"Mike." She cupped his cheek. "I mean this with the utmost kindness but you are a fucking idiot."

TWENTY-FOUR

Mike

REBECCA STRAVOKRAUS WAS A SHARK, a shark who was paid very well by the Gold to handle the media surrounding the team and, more specifically, the extra scrutiny that they received because of Brit.

Pierre Barie, Stefan's father and a powerful businessman in his own right, had snagged ownership of the team just over a year ago. Rebecca had been one of his first additions.

As a former publicist for a Hollywood starlet, media shit-shows were her specialty.

Mike just hoped she'd be up for this one.

It was after ten when she pulled through the gate and parked next to Stefan's car. He and Brit had arrived at the house first but hadn't made it past the foyer.

Now Rebecca *click-clicked* up the stairs and breezed past the four of them.

"Close the door," she chirped.

Mike shut the heavy panel and turned to escort everyone to the kitchen, but Sara had beaten him to it.

She'd gotten everyone seated on stools around the island. "What do you want to drink?"

"Nothing for me," Stefan said.

"I'll take a water if you have one," Brit said.

"Same for me," Rebecca said.

"Mike?" Sara asked.

He shook his head and watched as *his* woman opened a cabinet and grabbed three glasses, before filling them with ice and retrieving the pitcher of water from the fridge.

"I'm sorry to drag you guys out so late—"

Mike dropped his hand to Sara's waist and gave it a warning squeeze. "This isn't your fault—"

"Well, I guess that depends on how you determine fault," Rebecca said.

She spoke in such honey-sweet tones that it took Mike a second to process the words.

"Excuse me?" he snapped.

Cherry-red lips pursed before Rebecca brought her glass to her lips. "It depends on whether or not she cheated."

The air in the room froze.

"I don't think—" Brit began.

"I believe the public has already convicted and tried me on that fact," Sara said.

"But not this room," Mike said.

Rebecca set her glass on the counter. "Let's be frank here. This room doesn't mean a damn thing when it comes to the public's opinion."

Sara snorted but placed her hand on Mike's chest, quieting him when he would have spoken. "That's not exactly news, Ms. Stravokraus. I've lived through *public opinion*."

"The question isn't whether you've already navigated a media circus, but rather, whether or not you committed the crimes you've been accused of." Rebecca slipped her heels off her feet, sighing as they fell to the floor beneath her stool. "The truth may not matter to them, but it matters to me."

"I wish it were that easy."

"It *is* that easy."

"And if I cheated?"

Ruby-red lips curved. "I'd be hard-pressed to believe it." Rebecca bent and retrieved her iPad from her briefcase and swiped her finger across the screen.

A graph appeared, colored lines zigzagging across a white background.

"Your scores are in gold, Ms. Jetty." A fingernail painted the same shade of red as Rebecca's lips followed the metallic path. "I've traced these back to your first competitions and find it difficult to believe that you'd bribe the judges for the Westin Rink Winter Performance of 2002 or the 2003 Ms. Dairy Open or—"

"I know my scores, Ms. Stravokraus," Sara cut in. "What I don't understand is your reasoning for bringing them up."

"My reasoning is this. One." She ticked off her fingers as she spoke, little flashes of cherry in the soft lighting of the kitchen. "You could have been cheating since you were a child. Two. There's no payoff in that. Three. Your scores were consistently on a higher level than your age would seem to dictate. Four. You had no motivation to cheat because, five, you were infinitely more skilled than any other woman in that competition."

"Strange things happen in competitions all the time," Sara countered.

"You would have had to fall twice and shortened three of your jumps to match the difficulty level of the next closest girl."

Stefan whistled. "Is that true?"

Even Mike was taken aback. He'd known Sara was good but had his teenaged mind ever grasped *how* good?

"She was doing quads before most of the men were," Rebecca said and swiped her finger across the screen.

A video of Sara as she'd been, graceful legs and arms, but minimal womanly curves, appeared on the screen. She skated across the ice, quickly gaining speed before launching into the air.

One. Two. Three. Four—

Holy shit. It *was* true.

A crunch as she landed on one foot and jumped immediately again. Not another quad, but a double that she also stuck.

"This was practice the morning before the long program," Sara murmured.

"Yes."

Her waist lifted and fell under Mike's hand as she took a deep breath. "How do you know—"

"So much about you?" Rebecca made the iPad sleep and then folded her hands together. "I'm good at my job." A shrug that was paired with the slightest hint of pink on her elegantly made-up cheeks. "Also, I was a big fan."

Sara gave a self-deprecating smirk. "*Was,* I think, is the key word here." She waved away any response Rebecca might have made. "None of this is the point, however. I don't want my past to cloud the Gold's future. I know there was trouble with the press last season, and that the team is playing great right now. I —as Sara Jetty, disgraced figure skater—don't want to impact your chances."

Brit spoke up for the first time. "One thing I've learned is that hockey isn't more important than your happiness."

If Mike hadn't been so close to Sara, he might have missed her little hitch of breath.

"She's right, you know," he said. "At some point, hockey will be over for me, and I'll be left with—"

"Someone who might have taken that from you? Shit, Mike. How can I ask you to risk your career for me? For us?" She pulled away from him. "This is your dream. I should step back and let you live it."

"Sara." Brit slid from her stool and crossed around the island. "I know I'm just this strange chick who has no right to offer advice, but I'm pushy and bossy, and I'm going to offer it anyway, 'kay?"

Stefan choked back a laugh, and even Sara's lips twitched as she nodded.

"Hockey used to be my dream—my *only* dream—and the only thing I lived for. Same as, I suspect, skating was your life. But do you know what I found out once I was playing for the Gold?" She paused, and Sara shook her head. "That I wasn't sharing my life with anyone."

Brit glanced over at Stefan, and emotion was a heavy rope that connected them. "I discovered that going it alone was really lonely, and then I found Stefan, and things suddenly made sense." She blew out a breath, the sincerity in her tone making even Mike feel a little choked up.

Fucking feelings.

"Stefan was a risk. Hell," she said with a chuckle, "I was probably a bigger risk for him. But worse than the risk was the possibility of living a life without him."

"Shit, sweetheart," Stefan muttered, his eyes looking suspiciously glassy, "you're killing me."

Brit ran a finger under one eye as Stefan came around the island and pulled her into his arms. "Sorry, not sorry," she said, cupping his cheek. "There's no getting rid of me now."

"Not even a possibility," he said.

Sara sniffed, blinked rapidly.

"You two," Mike warned softly as he stepped close to his girl and wrapped an arm around her waist. "You make her cry and—"

"Tears aren't bad, Stewie," Brit said, turning in Stefan's

embrace and leaning her head back against his shoulder. "They remind us of what's important." A pause as her gaze connected with Sara's. "You understand?"

Sara sighed. "I do. But what about the team?"

Rebecca shoved her feet back into her heels and stood. "That's why I'm here."

TWENTY-FIVE

Sara

SARA WOKE UP SWEATING.

Which, she figured, was mainly due to Mike having curled around her like she was his favorite teddy bear.

Which wasn't a bad place to be, all things considered. Except for the sweating. And the need to pee.

Mornings after were new for her.

This being her second, both of which had featured Mike.

Men weren't regular fixtures in her life, and while she liked sex, she had always kept the sex part of her life and the sleeping part completely separate.

No walks of shame for her.

Carefully, she lifted Mike's arm from around her waist and wrestled herself free of the blankets.

His leg slung over the top of hers.

"Mike," she said, squirming. "I have to pee."

"Mmm." He rolled over, tucked her beneath him. She might have thought the stink was awake if not for his even breathing and clumsy sleep-stunted movements.

But it was like fighting an octopus, trying to get out of that bed.

She'd get one leg loose, and he'd toss his arm over her waist again. Then she'd wriggle free of that, and his leg would be back, shoving between hers and pinning her in place.

She was huffing and puffing and still sweaty by the time she managed to get out of the bed . . . or rather by the time she slipped off the edge of the mattress and fell to the floor in an ungraceful heap.

At which point—because this was her life—Mike decided to wake fully up.

"Problem?" he asked, rubbing his bare chest and yawning.

"Nope." Sara blew a strand of hair out of her face and hello, morning breath.

Toilet then toothbrush. STAT.

She flipped over, stood, and would have been in the bathroom if a hand on the back of her shirt hadn't caught and held her in place.

"Not running?"

"Nope." She crossed her legs, almost dancing in place.

"What happened to the girl who liked mornings?"

"She needs to pee." A pause, a huffed-out breath. "And to brush her teeth." The blankets rustled, and she felt herself being reeled back toward the bed. "I really need—"

"Shh." He turned her around, sitting up and positioning her between his thighs.

Brown eyes met hers. "You good?"

Her head dropped back, she sighed. "Mike—"

"You're good." His hands slid down and spanned her waist. Then they slid lower, beneath the hem of his t-shirt she'd commandeered in an effort to not have a repeat of their last morning after, and gripped her ass.

"Stop." She slapped his hands away. "Unless you're into something a lot more X-rated."

He smirked.

"And I don't mean bondage. I'm thinking more along the lines of golden showers—"

"Go." A tap to her bottom sent her on her way.

She hightailed it to the bathroom and closed the door. After using the facilities, she flushed and started to search the drawers for a spare toothbrush.

They'd crashed after Rebecca and company had left the night before, though not before bingeing a couple more episodes of *Game of Thrones*.

She might not completely understand the appeal of a fantasy world, but Khal Drogo, yeah. That was a man she could stare at all day.

Not finding a toothbrush in any of the vanity drawers, Sara turned to the linen closet set along the opposite wall.

"Crazy girlfriend antics already?"

Sara jumped, almost banging her head on the shelf she was bending over to peer at. "Do you not have a single spare toothbrush in here?" she asked, not taking the bait.

"Here." He opened a cabinet—which she'd skipped, because who kept spare toothbrushes beneath a sink?—and pulled out a pack. "Pink or green?"

"Green."

His breath caught as she snagged the brush and topped it with the toothpaste she'd found earlier.

"What?" she asked, though it sounded a lot more like "Shmut?"

He finished brushing his own teeth before straightening and leaning back against the vanity. "I just remembered that emeralds were your favorite."

She spit and rinsed in the sink then smiled at him. "Yes.

They still are, in fact. I can't believe you remember that." Her brows pulled down when he didn't smile back. "What is it?"

He was frozen, every muscle locked.

"Hey, Hot Shot." She touched his chest, and that ice around him melted. He moved abruptly, opening a drawer and tearing open a box of condoms then slipping away to turn on the shower. He pulled a stack of towels out from the linen closet. "Are—"

His boxer briefs dropped to the floor.

Her tongue stopped working.

"Come here."

An order. All male and tempting, kind of like the especially hard part of his anatomy bobbing her way.

But it wasn't his body that made her feet move.

His eyes.

Heat and desire and *need*. For her. If he'd looked at her like that earlier, she would never have been able to get out of bed, risk of golden shower or not.

Melted dark chocolate, his gaze dripped over her, warming her limbs, sticking to her insides, sliding down her inner thighs and making her knees tremble.

But she didn't need to worry about falling.

The moment she wavered, Mike was there, pulling her flush against his body and slamming his mouth down onto hers.

Sparks flew along her spine, spurred her into motion.

She kissed him back with everything she had, lips parting and tongue diving into his mouth.

The man made her insane.

He hitched her body up, grabbing her legs and wrapping them around his waist. His cock was hard between her thighs, making her desperate to shift her hips, to guide him deep inside.

But he wouldn't let her move.

His hands clamped on to her ass, and he turned them both.

Hot water cascaded down her back. It soaked into her hair, rolled down her arms, pooled between her breasts.

Moaning, she arched back, letting the drops drip lower.

"God, you're so fucking beautiful." Mike tucked one hand between her shoulders and adjusted her position so he could reach her nipple.

And fuck, that was good.

She hissed out a breath, then a groan, then a curse.

He switched to the other breast, repeated the circling of his tongue, the tease of his teeth. His scruff abraded her skin, but it was a good hurt, and she was so . . . very . . . close . . .

He tilted his hips, rubbed his cock up, against her clit and—

"Mike!"

She plummeted over the edge, stars exploding behind her eyes, pleasure spreading outward from her center.

And he rode her orgasm out with her, rubbing against her wetness, eliciting little aftershocks of pleasure with each up and down movement.

Sara could barely stand when he gently lowered her legs to the shower floor.

"Christ, I have to have you." She watched through lidded eyes as he reached for the condom he'd grabbed earlier and tore the wrapper open with his teeth.

Watching Mike fist his erection and stroke it from base to tip was just about the sexiest thing she'd ever seen. The laxness that had invaded her limbs evaporated, and she wanted it to be her hands there, *needed* his hard cock inside her.

"Hurry," she chanted. "Hurry. Hurry."

His fingers fumbled, and he dropped the condom. "Fuck, Sara. You're not helping. I've imagined you in my shower about a million times, and now you're in my life, and we're—"

And then it wasn't just about pleasure. It was about this

man and how much he meant to her, about her past and present colliding and moving forward.

Her eyes burned, but she blinked the tears back, not wanting to ruin what was supposed to be a happy moment. "I'm here, Mike. Finally, I'm here."

"Beautiful." He leaned in and kissed her. "Amazing." Pulled back and cupped her cheek. "The only woman I've ever wanted."

His words stole her breath, and he didn't give her time to get it back.

"The only woman," he said again then bent and retrieved the condom, sliding it on with suddenly sure fingers.

"Mike—"

He kissed the words from her lips. Hands hauled her up, spreading her thighs, and guiding her down . . . and, good God. Yes, she needed him *right there*.

Deep. Hard. Stretching her to capacity.

And pausing, her back pressed against the cold tile wall.

Why was he pausing?

"Look at me," he ordered.

She groaned, flexed her hips. He had to move. Right then or—

"Sara girl, *look* at me."

Her eyes opened, and the intensity in his gaze took her breath away. Or what little of it was left.

"You're mine." He pulled out. Slammed back in. Swiveled his hips and made her cry out. This was so much more than simple sensation. He made her ache with need and feel completely whole all in the same vein.

And she wanted more.

Out. In. Out. In. More—

"Say it."

She didn't need to ask what. She knew. It was the same

truth she'd held close for more than a decade. She would always be his.

"I'm yours."

His eyes slid closed. "Mine," he said.

"Yours." She grabbed his shoulders, yanked herself upright to growl in his ear. "And you're mine."

He chuckled, hot breath mixing with the water to raise goose bumps on her skin.

"Never been anyone else's."

The words spread through her, heightening the pleasure he was raising to a frantic peak.

"I'm going to—"

"Come for me, sweetheart."

As if her body would betray him. She exploded again, inner muscles clenching tightly against his cock and decimating his self-control.

He was a frenzy of movement, mouth on her breasts, her throat, her jaw, hips pounding into her. And then he was groaning against her neck as he climaxed, and she was wrapping her arms around him.

They stayed pressed together, not a molecule of air separating their bodies, as their breathing slowed, their pulses steadied.

He remained close as she washed her hair, rubbed a loofah gently across her back when it was time to soap up.

As the water began to cool, Mike turned if off and wrapped her in a towel.

They didn't speak. Words weren't necessary when their movements spoke volumes. A brush of his towel across her back, dabbing the scar there gently and soaking up the drops of water dotting her skin.

Her fingers combed through his hair, settling it just the way he liked it.

A thumb swiped beneath her eye to catch an errant tear.

Laced hands moved downstairs together. Two sets of lungs not breathing as they turned on the news. A stroke of his palm across her cheek when their pictures were the lead story.

"You're coming to the game tonight," he said after the anchor cut to commercial.

Sara nodded. "Okay."

"You're not alone anymore."

She forced her eyes from the screen when a picture of her on that podium, gold medal around her neck, came on. "I know."

"Jumping Bean." His tone was a warning.

"You know you only really use that nickname when you're getting all growly with me."

His face relaxed. "You like growly."

"Sometimes." She bumped her shoulder with his. "I'm also okay. You're here. That makes everything so much better."

He grinned. "Of course it does."

Her stomach growled, and she flicked off the TV. "What's for breakfast?" she asked before she caught the clock. "Or, I guess, lunch at this point."

Mike's nose wrinkled. "Chicken, rice, and greens with protein powder." He shuddered. "The team's nutritionist is strict as hell."

"She'd have to be to keep you boys in check."

"Hey!" he said, going to the freezer and opening the drawer. "Brit's the worst of the bunch."

"I've seen her body in real life. There's no way that's true."

He grinned. "Okay, it's a lie." He plunked a container of Phish Food on the counter. "But I also have this for you."

"An appetizer," she said, snatching the carton and opening a drawer to grab a spoon. "Perfect size for one."

He made to steal it from her, and she squeaked, but then he

nodded at her sketchpad. "Want to go on the patio and draw for a bit?" He pulled a Tupperware from the fridge. "I'll heat some of this up for us."

This man.

Her vision went slightly blurry around the edges, and her heart went all Grinch-like, feeling as though it had expanded by three sizes. "I like you, Mike Stewart."

"It's because I'm so likeable." He grinned then caught a glimpse of her eyes and sobered. "Together, remember?"

Blinking, she nodded. "Believe me, I remember." This time would be different. She'd wouldn't cave, and no way would she let it get as bad as it had been before. With a sigh, she straightened her shoulders and lifted her chin.

"Get to work, Hot Shot. I'm hungry."

TWENTY-SIX

Mike

MIKE SLIPPED OUT onto the patio, two plates of suitably healthy food in hand. Sunlight peeked through the clouds, creating pockets of gold around the deck. Sara's hair, the metal of the screws holding the boards in place, a reflection off—

A camera lens?

His neck crawled.

"Sara," he said.

"Mmm?" she asked, head still bent over the page.

He set the plates on the table and crossed the deck to kneel by her side, careful to keep his back to the place he'd seen the glare. "Jumping Bean."

She blinked, gaze sliding up to focus on his for a brief moment. He saw the urge in their depths, the desire to flick right back down to the sketch she was working on. "What's the matter?"

"I think I saw a camera."

Though her shoulders went ramrod stiff, Sara didn't lose her composure. "Where?"

"To the east, behind that big oak toward the back of the property."

Blue eyes searched the space behind him before returning back to his. "I think you're right."

God, she was amazing. Given her history, she should be a blubbering mess right now. Instead she sat there, regal as a queen, face calm, words calmer still.

"So, the question is," she said, her tone surprisingly light, "do we give them their shot? Or keep the masses frenzied and waiting?"

He leaned close and pressed a kiss to her forehead. "We only give what we're willing."

Standing, he reached for her hand, tugged her to her feet. "Now, let's go inside and have lunch away from the prying eyes."

He was also going to make some calls and see about getting security for his property. A gate had always been enough of a deterrent for anyone before. That had obviously changed.

"Eating from inside a fishbowl isn't relaxing before your game?" she teased.

"Not exactly." Mike smiled, but it wasn't completely genuine. And his tone was off. Because . . . *goddammit*, he hated this. Despised that Sara even had to go through it at all.

But she misread his frustration.

Blue eyes clouded with sorrow, her shoulders fell a fraction of an inch. "I'm sorry you're dealing with this."

He wanted to pull her close, but he didn't want an audience for that.

So instead, he dropped her hand, picked up their plates, and opened the French door to the kitchen, nodding at her to enter. Following after her, he bumped his elbow against a switch on the wall on his way in.

Immediately, the windows darkened as the remote-controlled shades slid down.

The plates were on the countertop in the next instant. "Come here," he said, but didn't give her the chance to respond. He crossed to her, hauled her into his chest, and wrapped his arms tight. "No apologies. Not ever. This is not your fault."

She snorted. "Kind of is."

"Yeah no. That's bullshit, and you know it." Mike slid one hand up and cupped her cheek, forced her to focus on him. "It's bullshit."

Sara sighed. "I'm trying to feel sorry for myself here."

Lips twitching, he tucked her hair behind her ear. "Not happening. Not in my house."

"In your—" A huff. "You're such a caveman."

"Aw," he teased, tugging that strand of hair. "You're so cute when you try to be tough."

"Try?" She crossed her arms and glared. "I don't have to—"

God, he loved her.

It was nearly impossible to smother the urge to make the declaration, but he knew it wasn't the right time, didn't want the moment he finally confessed how he'd felt for the last ten years to be marred by the outside world.

Instead, he kissed her, and when her body melted, he took advantage of having known the girl for so long.

Fingers slipping up, he trailed them along the sides of her breasts. She moaned, and he went in for the kill.

Her armpits.

Digging into the spot, her *only* ticklish spot, Mike had no mercy.

She squealed, mouth breaking away, body squirming so violently that he almost lost his grip.

But he was a professional athlete, and his reaction time was on point.

"You"—she gasped—"are—so dead!"

Her hands lurched up and gripped his hips. He turned, but not in time, and her fingers found the spot on his waist.

"Shit!"

"Payback," she said, smirking as she broke free.

One brow came up. "Payback, really?"

Sprinting around the side of the island, she positioned herself so that it was between them.

But the barrier was nothing.

Still, he let her think that she was safe . . . for the moment.

"You know I hate being tickled."

A step forward. A slide of one barstool slightly to the right.

There. Now he had a clear shot.

Sara leaned forward, plucked a piece of broccoli from the plate, and stuck it in her mouth.

He waited while she chewed, not wanting her to choke, but when she reached for another bite and said, "So, yes, payback and—" She shrieked when he launched himself over the island, and he loved the sound, loved surprising her, loved . . .

Her.

His mouth crashed down on hers, his hands slid under the hem of her shirt, and the chicken was very cold by the time they settled down to eat it.

"REMIND me why I let you talk me into this again?" Sara grumbled.

"You'll be fine. Remember, you're charming, and the WAGs are nice."

That wasn't a lie, thankfully, because he'd played on a few teams where the opposite was true.

"Charming," she muttered, slinging her purse on her shoulder. "I still can't believe that Mitch won't let me work."

"He said the store is a shit-show, and he was keeping it closed for the rest of the week because he was tired of people coming in and not buying anything except your stuff." The three pieces she'd given to her boss had apparently sold out within an hour of opening.

"I'm sure people are just going to burn them. Or amplify every single imperfection." She reached for the door leading out to the garage.

He snagged her arm. She huffed. He smiled. It was kind of their thing.

"We need to go, Mike. Traffic—"

"What's going on, cranky pants?"

"I tolerate a lot of your nicknames, but—"

He kissed her, felt her body relax for a half second. At least until she seemed to remember they were bickering and pulled away.

Damn, he'd have to work on that.

"Don't change the subject," he said when she opened her mouth, probably to bitch him out. While he didn't want to fight with her, he wanted her to be able to confide in him, not bottle it up. "What's got you as ornery as a pissed-off cat?"

"What in hell are you talking about?"

"Sara." He pressed her back against the door, not stopping until she had to tilt her head back to look—or rather, *glare* —at him.

"It's nothing."

"It's something."

She sighed. He smiled because, even though he'd rather be having naked fun time with her, every moment with Sara was a good one.

Two hands came up, shoved at his chest. Not that the action budged him an inch.

"Mike." Another sigh.

"I can stay here all day."

Sara shook her head, but her lips were finally curving, and the irritation in her expression slipped away. "I bet you could."

"Did I not give you enough orgasms today?"

Her mouth dropped open, and he had to resist the urge to kiss it, to thrust his tongue inside and—

"I don't think there's such a thing." She gave him the smile, the trademark Sara Jetty grin, except this one reached her eyes.

She was smiling from the inside out.

He puffed up, couldn't help it. Especially when she said, "And no, that's not the problem, Hot Shot. You gave me plenty."

Nuzzling into her neck, he asked, "Then what?"

"I'm nervous."

"This is you nervous?" One of her legs had come up, wrapped around his knee.

Shit. He wanted to hitch it higher, to push her pants down and his fingers inside her wet heat. He—

—stepped back.

"You get horny when you're nervous?"

A wry smirk. "Apparently."

"Come on, Trouble," he said, lacing his hand with hers, the other adjusting his situation south of the border. At this rate, they could hire him to hammer nails into that wall the president wanted to build. "I'll give you the gossip on the drive, make you feel like you're part of the crowd before you even get there and have to hear it all over again."

"Again with the nicknames." She shook her head but followed him to her car. "You're incorrigible."

"That's why you love me," he teased as he opened the passenger side door.

Fuck. He realized what he'd said when she froze halfway into the car.

"Shit, sweetheart. I'm sorry. I was joking. Don't worry about it." He was rambling, couldn't seem to stop. "I—"

She straightened. "Here's the thing." A deep breath. "I think I do love you. That's part of what makes this so hard. The last time I cared about something as much as you, I screwed it up." Her voice broke. "I don't want to ruin us, Mike."

His heart swelled so big it could have been a balloon, a ball of helium right on the precipice of too much air, just about to burst.

"Sit down, Sara girl. There's something I want to show you."

When she didn't move, he gently pushed her shoulder down and lifted her legs into the car. He closed the door then walked around the hood and slid into the driver's seat.

Silence. Complete and utter silence greeted him, but he knew that before he said anything else that he had to show her.

Had to make her understand.

The glove compartment opened with a soft *click,* and he reached inside, shifting the registration and proof of insurance to the side. Because beneath that was a box.

A box he'd had for a really long time.

"I don't know if you know this, but I came to your house two nights before you were supposed to leave."

Sara turned her head, eyes wide and damp with tears. "You did?"

Her voice, steady, calm, laced with hurt, gave him the courage to go on. She was strong, but she also needed to know. And just as important, he needed her to grasp exactly how deep his feelings went.

"Yes. At that point we'd spent two years in a car together, five mornings a week. More than five-hundred hours by ourselves, and I was ridiculously in love with you."

"Was?"

He nodded, hating the way she curled in on herself when he spoke. "Was. But at the same time, I didn't want to interrupt your training, I'd convinced myself to wait until you came back from Italy. Then I got the call."

"Juniors."

"Yeah. I went to the store. It was ridiculously stupid, I see that now, but I—" He gritted his teeth, pressed on. "I picked this out. Had this notion that I'd give it to you as a promise. Your parents were there and they made me understand just how stupid of an idea it was."

"My parents?"

"They were right. You didn't need any more distractions, least of all from me and my family." Mike yanked at his tie. "Hell, I was all ready to argue with them, and then I got another call."

Her hand rested on his thigh for a second. "What call?"

"The police had busted my mom. She got caught trying to buy OxyContin from an undercover cop." He laughed, and it was bitter. His family had cost him so much. "She needed detox and rehab, and I didn't need to bring that shit into your life."

"I would have been there for you."

"I know you would have." Turning, he stared at her, beautiful even in the pale light of the garage. "I wouldn't have let you, and your parents were right. You didn't need my family messing up your chances. It didn't matter anyway. You were gone, and by the time I got everything sorted so I could leave town too, I was ready to leave it all behind." He tapped the box against his leg. "Thing is, I was convinced then that you were better off without me. Hell, all this current bullshit is because of *my* mom, so the logic is there—"

"That's not—"

"Shh. I'm too selfish to live without you again. You make me feel whole, Sara girl. I've loved you since that first morning in my car, and nothing is going to change the way I feel." He opened the box and held it out. "And the thing is, I think you could use an ally at your back."

She glanced down at the ring, and he winced. He should have had it cleaned, or added a giant diamond or something. Instead, it was just the same as it had always been.

A simple silver band, a trio of small emeralds.

"I . . . uh . . . I—don't—"

Fuck. He was fucking this up. Quickly, he closed the lid. "I'll get you something different."

"It's not that. I"—she blew out a breath—"I'm confused."

He was proposing, and the woman in front of him was confused.

"It's okay," he said, the words rushed as he shoved the box into the glove compartment and slammed it closed. "We can talk about it later."

He started the car and began backing out of the garage, had to slam on the brakes when he realized he hadn't hit the opener.

"Mike."

"Later." The door rattled up, and he zipped down the driveway.

Fuck, but he wanted to hit someone.

Luckily he could do that on the ice.

TWENTY-SEVEN

Sara

HOLY SHIT, had that been a proposal?

Dumbstruck, Sara stared out the window as Mike navigated his car down the driveway and through the gate.

It couldn't have been a proposal.

That didn't make any sense, not yet—

Flashes blinded her as they pulled into the street.

"Fuck," Mike muttered, swinging wide to avoid the paparazzi on the sidewalk. The group of men in dumpy sweatshirts and torn jeans crowded near the car, shoving those black lenses up to the windows, clicks echoing through the glass.

"Make sure the gate closes," she murmured, when he started to drive away before it had shut the last few feet.

A nod, though he didn't respond with words. Then the gate was barred, and they were speeding down the road. They'd hit the freeway and the typical 101 slowdown, silence reigning in the car before Sara wrapped her mind around the fact—

"You proposed?"

Male shoulders hunched. Big, strong hands that could touch

so gently clenched so tightly on the steering wheel that it creaked in protest.

"Not exactly."

"Then want to tell me what that was?"

A car cut in front of them, and Mike muttered a curse. "Stupidity?"

She sighed. "Want to try again?"

"Not really."

Well, clearly this was getting her nowhere. She reached for the glove compartment and pushed the button to open it.

"Don't."

Too late.

Her fingers found the soft velvet box and extracted it. The brass hinges made a little squeak when she opened the lid. "This is an engagement ring."

Eyes flicked to hers then back to the road. "It wasn't intended as one. Not then." She opened her mouth, but he spoke before she could ask what the hell *that* meant. "I wanted to give you a promise ring. I wasn't stupid enough to think we were old enough to marry."

Her heart pounded. Mike had wanted to give her a promise for more.

Holy flipping shit-on-a-stick.

In the two years he'd driven her to practice, she had never thought he'd noticed her as anything more than an obligation. He'd been borrowing her parents' car, after all. Oh, they'd had some good times together, shared many a laugh about his teammates and her coaches, once they'd gotten past his early morning grouchiness, but he'd never touched her.

Like not ever.

Except, her mind didn't let that lie stick.

She remembered him hugging her when she'd had a terrible practice and ended up bruised and bloodied, having landed hard enough on her knee to tear through fleece legging and skin alike.

He'd rolled her bag to the car for her when her hands ached from the frigid cold rink.

He'd helped her into the passenger seat when she'd twisted her ankle.

A hundred examples of his caring flew through her mind. She remembered what she'd blocked away, what she hadn't understood as a young and inexperienced teenager.

Her love had come in the form of a Minnesota Wild sweatshirt, in homemade cookies, a quick sketch of his team's logo—and not a very good one at that.

She stared at the emeralds, watched them twinkle in the late afternoon sunlight. They were small by today's standards, but that didn't mean any less to her heart. "Why did you give me the ring today?"

Mike jumped, and Sara realized that she'd been inside her head for a while, long enough that they were turning into the parking lot for the rink.

The car slowed; the window whirred down a crack. Which was enough to hear a cacophony of shouts and yells, shutters clicking, and faintly, a male voice, "Go straight through, Mr. Stewart. Security has you covered."

With a *snick*, the sound was gone, and they moved forward again.

Another gate. More reporters.

And then quiet.

Was it possible for a parking lot to give her nostalgia?

Because this one was. The slightly worse-for-wear metal door, the mix of SUVs and sedans, albeit of a nicer breed than those from her childhood rink.

"I haven't been to an ice rink since—"

Mike parked the car, shut off the engine, and faced her. The frustration seemed to bleed out of him, replaced with understanding and compassion.

"Well, this one is a little bigger than ours at home."

"I bet that's what all the boys say." Her smile was tremulous.

He reached out an arm, pressed his thumb to her bottom lip. "I want you in my life, Sara girl." A brush of his mouth against hers. "Know I'll take you any way I can get you."

Leaning back, he unbuckled her seatbelt.

"And the ring?" she asked, for some reason slightly breathless.

"It means whatever you want it to," he said, opening his door and stepping out.

"Whatever I—?"

Mike popped her door and gestured toward the rink. She shoved the ring into her pocket and trailed after him, absolutely bewildered.

Whatever she wanted it to mean.

Fuck, and men said *women* were complicated.

"Hey!"

This time it wasn't a mob of men shouting at Sara, but a single female voice, and a familiar one at that.

"Brit," she said and slowed.

The Gold's starting goalie strode confidently across the parking lot in a silk blouse, blazer, and jacket. She wore heeled pumps and looked like a model's take on a powerful attorney.

Mike whistled. "Looking good, Plantain."

"Shut it, Stewie." She punched his arm.

"It's true," he said, opening the door and holding it for them. "I've never seen you look so—"

"I'd be very careful about how you finish that sentence, Hot Shot," Sara chimed in.

Brit cackled. There was no other word for it, just exploded into evil laughter.

"You breathe one—"

"Don't bother with threats, *Hot Shot*." Blue eyes cut to Sara's. "You have more embarrassing material to provide me with, right?"

"Loads."

More laughter, this time from both of them.

Mike groaned. "I was trying to give you a compliment."

Brit got herself together. She reached up—because even though she was tall for a woman, Mike was still taller—and patted his cheek. "I know. I'm touchy because Stefan got me a personal shopper."

"He *what?*"

Her eyes rolled up. "It's not entirely his fault. I complained about not knowing what to wear, since I didn't really do the suit thing, and he's a man."

Seeing that Mike didn't follow the sentiment, Sara explained. "She had a problem. Stefan went all caveman and wanted to fix it." She touched his arm and softened her tone. "It's kind of what you guys do."

"Exactly!" Brit said. "So I couldn't be mad at him and anyway"—she patted her hips—"I think it works."

"Plus, those shoes," Sara said.

"These shoes." Brit sighed happily.

Mike frowned as he glanced down at her feet. "What about the shoes?"

They were pointed, a polished metallic black with specks of gold. They were also totally killer, with a burnished metal heel and bright red soles.

Sara sighed too. "You'd never understand."

"Apparently not," he said and captured her hand. "Now come on. I'll show you where you can hang out until after the game."

They called their good-byes to Brit, and Mike led Sara to an elevator.

As the doors slid closed, a thought occurred to her. "Don't NHL teams usually have a separate practice rink?"

"Left field, much?"

"Not exactly," she said. "But I remember skating at Nationals. It was on the Blues' home ice, and I feel like all of their practice stuff wasn't at the arena, but at a smaller rink nearby."

"It's true. Sometimes the team will have a pregame skate on the big ice, but the rest of the practices are held elsewhere. The Gold are different. Or at least for the rest of this season." He pushed a button to select the floor. "Barie's father is building a rink, but it took some time to secure the land and permits, I guess."

"Why not just continue to practice here?"

"Bad business," he said. "Our former owners were real fuckups, to be honest. They embezzled money, made questionable financial decisions, negotiated with players using underhanded techniques. Arenas make money from concerts and other events."

Oh. That made sense.

"If there are no events, then use the facility, but the Gold Mine is in a prime spot of San Francisco." A shrug. "The owners don't make money from our practices. They'd be much better off filling the stands with Beyoncé fans."

"The Beyhive in the Gold Mine."

He snorted. "Something like that."

"So a practice rink?"

"They're doing a huge multi-sheet skating center. It's good press, and the Bay Area is in desperate need of ice."

The elevator doors dinged open, and Sara let Mike lead her down the hallway. "Why so big? It's California, not Minnesota, after all."

A nudge of his elbow. "Wouldn't let the powers that be hear you say that, sweetheart. Hockey is up and coming in California, and San Jose actually has the largest adult hockey program in the States."

She tried to correlate that in her mind. Ocean waves, redwoods, flip-flops and cargo shorts and tree huggers.

"I can hear your mind working from here." His hand slid up her back to tug her ponytail. "Trust me on the need and want."

Wasn't Kristi Yamaguchi from San Francisco? Or nearby? She'd never really put two and two together before, but really, she'd lived in the city for five years. She should know better.

Northern California was *not* Southern California.

It kind of had seasons, if summer in San Francisco could be considered a season. And it even rained and stuff.

She snorted, and Mike's fingers slipped to the back of her neck. He kneaded the muscles there as he turned them down a hallway.

"Care to share with the class?" he asked, eyes twinkling. He'd obviously put the earlier ring debacle away for the present and—

Dear God, she didn't need to be thinking about *that* right now.

Later. Rings and maybe proposals she would put off to think about until later.

"Just that you'd better come get me after the game. I'm thoroughly turned around."

"Bwahaha!" he mock-evil-laughed. "My plan is working."

A smack to his chest. "You're a dork."

"And you're here."

They stopped in front of a nondescript door. A panel was on the wall outside it, one of those placards that gave the name and number. Mike didn't give her a chance to read it.

He turned the knob, and they walked straight into chaos.

TWENTY-EIGHT

Mike

MIKE WAS USED to the sight and sound of a dozen women talking and laughing in the Family Suite—their voices echoing off the walls, mingling with the sound of several blaring televisions as well as the clinking of silverware against plates, music playing in the background, toy cars being run across countertops, but Sara flinched as he tugged her across the threshold.

A blip of silence trailed their entrance as twenty-something eyes flicked in their direction then away before the conversation started back up.

The sound of the Matchbox cars rolling along the granite abruptly cut off, and little feet pounded in their direction.

"What did you bring me, Mr. Mike?" a little girl who barely came up to his waist asked.

Mirabel was the daughter of their backup goalie, Spence, and as gorgeous as her model mother. Black corkscrew curls, coffee skin, chocolate eyes, bright white teeth and a brilliant smile.

"Nothing today, pipsqueak," he told her.

Her bottom lip came out, and he grinned, well familiar with the young girl's tactics.

"Mirabel," her mother, Monique, warned.

"How about I have Brit make some good saves?"

Rosebud lips pressed together, considering.

"And," he whispered as he crouched down, "this." He slid a chocolate kiss into her hand.

"Mike," Monique said, now warning him. "You'll spoil her."

He tugged one of Mira's springy curls. She unwrapped the chocolate and shoved it in her mouth before her mother could confiscate it.

Smart girl.

"She's the only kid around," he said. "She needs spoiling."

The Gold were a young team, and Mira was the only kid amongst the WAGs. Their players were either single, or those who were in committed relationships didn't have kids yet.

"More will be coming soon and then—"

"She'll lead the shenanigans." Mike winked, teasing a smile out of Monique. "I wanted to introduce you to someone. This is—"

"Sara Jetty, as I live and breathe."

Sara's face paled, and Mike didn't blame her. Monique's tone was completely unreadable. Still, he had to give his girl credit. She didn't flinch or shy away, just extended a hand.

"Nice to meet you . . ."

"Monique LeBrat," she said. "Spence's wife."

Sara flicked her gaze in his direction. "Backup goalie," he said.

"Sorry," Sara murmured. "I haven't been watching the team for long, and I'm not totally familiar with the players." She gave a self-deprecating laugh. "I've kind of avoided everything to do with the ice since . . . well, you know."

Monique tilted her head. "Since the *you know*."

"Yup. *You knows* are painful, if you would believe it."

"You know?" Monique tapped one black painted fingernail against her mouth. "I think I would."

Sara giggled.

"All right," Monique said and slid an arm around Sara's shoulders, tugging her away from Mike. "Come on, and let me introduce you around. I'll even tell you where they store the really good chocolate."

"You good, Sara girl?" He didn't like leaving her, but he also didn't want to mess up her chances of making a friend or two up here. The WAGs were super protective of the team, and once they accepted someone into their fold, it was for life.

Sara had made a good start already and didn't need him hanging around cramping her style.

"She's good," Monique said, pulling her into the other room and making a shooing motion. "Go do your hockey thing. We're going to get to know each other."

But Mike didn't move, not until Sara's eyes connected with his, and she nodded.

He probably wouldn't have gone even then, except her expression was anticipatory, as though she wanted the chance to know the girls.

"I'll meet you up here after the game."

"Good luck," she said softly and let Monique lead her into the next room of the suite.

THEY WERE DOWN two goals in the bottom of the third with seventeen seconds to go.

The crowd was pouring out of the arena, the fair-weather fans leaving to beat the rush while the diehards stayed on.

Hockey was a game of seconds, but they were quickly running out of them.

At the sound of the ref's whistle, Mike skated to the blue line and readied himself for the faceoff. They were in the offensive zone, with an extra attacker—Coach had just pulled Brit—but they needed to act fast if they were going to make a game of it.

The Gold needed a goal *now*.

And then another.

Music from the arena's speakers cut off, the ref stood between the players, telling them to adjust their sticks, their feet, and—

The puck dropped.

It was a clean win—meaning their center was able to send the puck exactly where he wanted it, in this case to Mike, before the other center even touched it. Mike flicked it to Barie, who in a set play, passed it right back to him for a one-timer.

Blue crashed the net and . . . deflected the puck just enough that it squeaked between the goalie's pads.

Goal!

But he and the boys hardly celebrated. They had more work to do. The season was winding down, and every single point counted.

Line back up at center ice. Ten seconds left on the clock. Setup for the faceoff and . . . go!

This time the puck landed on Barie's stick. He carried it forward, Mike sliding back and middle to cover his position. Blue streaked up the boards, and Stefan spotted him, sending a lofting pass cross-ice to land right on his tape. A deke, a rapid change in direction paired with an acceleration, and it was just the rookie and their opponent's goalie.

Seconds ticked down. Four. Three. Two—

Score!

The remaining fans were louder than the entire arena had been all night, jumping to their feet and screaming as he and the guys mobbed Blue.

Two goals, fifteen seconds. That had to be a record.

They skated to the bench as Brit returned to her net. Another puck drop, and the buzzer sounded.

The game would be decided in overtime . . . or a shootout.

Coach said a few things, but not many. His words of wisdom mostly came in practice rather than the games, which he believed were the time for execution. Tweaks would be made, but primary system changes were to be cultivated during practice.

Overtime was three on three, and Mike would be on the ice with Blue and Blane, following Stefan's trio.

In close games, the bench was shortened—meaning, Coach gave the hot and more experienced players more ice time.

Luckily, that included him.

Winners wanted the puck. And he was definitely a winner—

And great, now he sounded like Keanu from the bad football movie, *The Replacements*. But his lips twitched when he wondered if Sara had seen it—

Tweet!

He pushed all extraneous thoughts away and focused on the game.

Players streaked across the ice, now with so much more space since each team was down two players. Six instead of ten skaters made for more room, more excitement, more goals.

Stefan peeled off and came hard to the bench. Mike jumped over the boards when he got close and rushed forward to join the play. He picked up a pass, got a shot on goal that deflected into the corner. Seeing that the forwards were tired, he hustled over and snagged the puck.

That gave the rest of Stefan's group time to change . . . and Blue the chance to get back on the ice.

The kid was on a run right now, and Mike wanted to get him the puck.

He turned, skated toward the front of the net, but instead of going for the shot like everyone no doubt expected, he made a quick move and dropped the biscuit to Blue.

Who wound up, shot, and—*fuck*—hit him right in the ass.

There was a reason players weren't supposed to have their backs to the net.

But what made his aching cheek feel better was the offending disk landing right between his feet. He reacted, flicking the puck up and over the goalie's shoulder.

The red light came on. The buzzer sounded.

And hell yeah, *that* felt good.

TWENTY-NINE

Sara

SARA WAS COMFORTABLY TUCKED into one of the ridiculously plush armchairs of the Family Suite reading on her phone and waiting for Mike to finish his post-game routine.

Monique had left a few minutes earlier to take Mirabel home—it was a school night after all—and the others had gone after the game, since they'd brought their own cars.

Sara had been surprisingly relaxed with the women in the suite that night. A couple had given her a curious look when they'd recognized her name and face, but none had been cruel or asked her any questions about her past.

What was going on between her and Mike was a different story.

Apparently, relationships were a hot topic.

Still, she kept things light; telling them how she and Mike had run into each other after so long apart and just hit it off. They'd laughed hysterically at the rain-car-blocking-traffic story, which she had to admit was kind of funny now.

Kind of.

Monique was definitely the most welcoming, and Sara hoped that they would continue to get along.

It would be nice to have some female friends.

The row of televisions on the wall were black, the lights dimmed. Three separate spaces made up the suite: the large open area with TVs to watch the game, another that held a kitchen and a play zone for the kids, er, *kid*, since Mirabel was the only munchkin around, and a bathroom.

The suite was beautifully decorated in pale gold with accents of black and white, and she found herself drifting off under the logo-emblazed fleece blanket that was pulled up to her chin.

She let her eyes slide closed after reading the same paragraph three times over.

"Hey."

"Mmm." She shifted, almost found herself on the floor.

"Careful." Mike placed his hands on her arms and gently nudged her back. "Sorry I took so long."

Sara glanced at the phone in her hand, saw that it was not quite midnight. "I thought you'd be later." The blanket fell as she stretched and sat up. His eyes flicked down to her breasts, and those little hussies perked to immediate attention. "Nice goal."

A flash of white teeth. "You saw?"

"Of course." She stood. "That's what I was here for."

"I thought maybe it was the wine."

Her cheeks felt a little pink. So, there'd been a little wine to go with the girl talk, but the gossip had mostly stopped when the game came on.

Hockey was serious business in these parts, and the wives and girlfriends fiercely cheered on the entire team.

"Shh." She walked into his arms, stood on tiptoe, and kissed the hell out of him.

Though she'd wanted to knock his socks off and knew they had no shortage of chemistry, the heat that swept through her was almost shocking. It began in her middle, radiating outward to her limbs.

She was on fire—

"You're dangerous, sweetheart," Mike murmured, pulling back to cup her face. He pressed his mouth to hers in a chaste kiss. "Dangerous for my sanity." His smile softened the words. "Ready?"

"Take me home, Hot Shot."

He slung an arm over her shoulder. "Now *that's* a sentiment I can get behind."

THE FRONT GATE of Mike's house was still crowded with paparazzi, but they slid through the barrier barely stopping.

"Wait for—"

"I hired some security. They'll make sure it's closed."

Her head twisted toward him. "When could you have possibly found the time to hire security?"

He shrugged. "A former teammate runs a management firm. He has connections and hooked me up."

"What management firm?"

"Prestige Media Group."

"*Prestige?*" She tried to control her shock, really she did. It still sounded like a shriek though.

"Um, yes?"

Why did Mike sound so confused? How could he be so calm when—

"Devon Scott is your former teammate?"

The garage door rolled open, and Mike pulled the car inside. "Yes." He was amused now.

"*The* Devon Scott."

"I don't know about *the*"—he did air quotes with his fingers—"Devon Scott. Dev used to play for the Gold, but that was before I came to the team. We overlapped for a season on the Kings."

"That's when he dated . . ."

"Emily Perkins. Yup." He rolled his eyes. "And if we're comparing media circuses. . ."

"I love her movies. I wonder—"

"He's married now. Not to a movie star."

Her shoulders dropped. "Oh." A pause. "I'd still like to meet him."

"What, am I second best?" He turned off the car, pushed the remote for the garage door.

"He has dreamy chocolate eyes."

"Dream—" Mike shook his head, expression irritated. "*He's married.*"

She couldn't resist pushing his buttons. "And he was still voted 2009's Sexiest Man Alive."

"I think his wife might have something to say about that," Mike muttered, reaching for the handle.

"I also think you're adorable when you're jealous."

He froze, brows pulling down.

"And when you frown."

The corner of his mouth twitched.

"And I think your eyes are way more dreamy."

A full smile. "And I think you are way more trouble than I gave you credit for."

"People underestimate me."

Those dreamy eyes went a little serious. "Yes. Yes, they do."

"No sappy," she warned, holding her hands up, palms out. "I've had enough serious for a while. Let's stick with fun."

"Fun as in you teasing me?"

She shrugged and got out. "Yes, that works."

"Or fun as in sexy naked time?" he asked, getting out and looking over the top of the car at her. The garage was dark, except for the faint light coming from the opener above their heads.

He was gorgeous, as in he *literally* took her breath away, all planes of hard lines softened by his five o'clock shadow and plump lips.

She wanted to sketch him.

She wanted to fuck him more.

"I do like sexy naked time." Sara tugged at the hoodie she'd borrowed from him. It was huge and baggy, but she hadn't exactly packed a bunch of clothes when she'd left her apartment.

She'd need to go over, get a few things if they were going to stay here, and with the group camped outside of the gate, that seemed to be the only reasonable possibility.

"I know you do." Mike grinned, and it was predatory.

Thoughts of the paparazzi faded because *God*, did she love the way he looked at her, eyes smoldering, focus intense. Every inch of the huge, muscular body was tuned into her.

And she wanted every inch inside her.

Her mouth quirked.

He raised a brow.

"Just making up bad innuendos to myself." She gave a self-deprecating chuckle. "Inches. And—" Two steps back, and she was next to the workbench. She picked up a random piece of pipe. What it was doing there, she had no idea. But it served her purpose. "Shaft." The tape measure she held up next. "Length."

Mike snorted, but those dreamy eyes were on fire, and those flames shot straight between her thighs.

Her lips parted, her exhale was shaky—

Then he was there, lifting her on top of the workbench,

stepping between her thighs. "And let me guess—" A thrust of his hips, grinding that hard erection against her. "You need to use my *tool?*"

She burst out into giggles, the whole scenario almost too ridiculous for words. "I love you."

His face went soft. "Me too, sweetheart. So much." Then he grinned, wicked and promising. "But no more sap, remember?" He unzipped her hoodie, tossed it to the side.

She ripped his shirt from his slacks, slid her hands over the exposed flesh. "How about hard and fast instead?"

"Hard, I can do," he said, mouth dropping to her neck, hands finding the button of her jeans and tugging down the zipper. "Fast, not so much."

Sara undid the waistband of his pants, gripped him tight. "I think you can do fast, Hot Shot."

"Fuck," he groaned.

A stroke. Another and . . . Mike showed her he could do fast.

THIRTY

Mike

IF HIS AND Sara's first night together after the press got hold of their story had been nearly perfect (and it had been, since Mike was pretending the proposal debacle hadn't happened), then the next two weeks became progressively less so.

The media attention was frenzied.

Twice more, photographers had hopped the back fence to his property and had to be escorted off with threats of criminal trespassing charges if they returned.

The circus outside his gate grew, as did the complaints from his neighbors.

Not that he blamed them. The fucking paparazzi were imposing and annoying as hell, but what was Mike supposed to do? The team was in the middle of the season, and he *had* to be in the area.

And he wasn't about to be separated from Sara, at least not any sooner than the team's schedule pulled him away.

Plus, it was safer.

He had employed three full-time security guards, and

enough cameras had been installed to keep an eye on big brother himself.

But now the press was affecting the team.

Sara paced back and forth in front of the television tuned into the gossip show. Blue had been out with a few of the guys, and several belligerent photographers had tried to get a reaction by calling Sara unkind names.

They'd gotten one.

In the form of Blue throwing a punch.

Not that Mike hadn't felt like doing the same when he'd heard the C-word in reference to *his* woman, but it wasn't Blue's battle to fight.

"He shouldn't put his career at risk," Sara said, stopping to stare at the TV. Her shoulders slumped. "Not for me."

"It wasn't for you." Mike crossed to her, placing his hands on those slumped shoulders and forcing her to look at him. "Or at least not you specifically. Blue is a good kid. The team is full of good guys. Not one of us would tolerate that about a teammate's spouse."

"But—"

"Not one." He pressed a soft kiss to her lips. "We just need to ride this out."

Sara opened her mouth to respond but was interrupted by the doorbell.

Since the security team hadn't called up to the house, it had to be either Brit, Stefan, or Rebecca.

Given the video running on repeat, he suspected the later.

His suspicion was confirmed at the second chime of the bell as he strode to the door. Rebecca then. She was nothing if not impatient.

And lived on her phone.

"Yes, Devon. I know," she snapped as she strode through the

door, cell to her ear. "We've been behind this thing from the beginning. It's *all* fucking damage control."

All righty then. Mike closed the front door, followed Rebecca into the kitchen.

Sara was perched on a stool, her pencil in hand as she sketched rapidly. He might as well order an entire a box of notebooks at the rate she was filling them.

She didn't appear to notice or hear Rebecca's cellular ranting. Either that, or she was way better at ignoring the publicist than he was. He closed the distance between them and peeked over her shoulder.

Circles on top of circles filled the page. They were intersected with harsh, radiating lines, amorphous figures hidden in the shadows.

He knew immediately what she'd drawn.

They were huddled in his front yard.

Rebecca tossed her phone on the counter, making Sara jump. The pencil hit the ground, but Rebecca didn't seem to notice.

"Dang, girl," she said. "Rumor had it that you could actually draw, but this"—she snagged the sketchpad—"*these* are good. Like really good." Her red nails were in stark contrast to the gray scale drawings as she flipped through the pages. "Oh, this is perfect. I can see it. Instagram. These. Drawings of the team."

Rebecca grabbed her phone and took a bunch of pictures of Sara's sketches before typing frantically into her phone. Then it was back at her ear.

"Do you see those, Devon?" Her voice was positively gleeful now. "Think of how well they'll translate to Instagram. Yes. *Yes.* Exactly. Okay, I'll set it up. Bye."

The phone landed back on the island.

Holy tornado.

"What's going on Rebecca?"

"The usual shit-show, but I think we finally have a way out."

"Through Instagram," Sara muttered dryly.

"Yes." Rebecca turned and began pacing. "It's perfect because you're not on any form of social media—" Her head whipped around and fixed Sara with a glare. "You're not, right? Not even under a fake name?"

"No."

Mike slipped behind her, putting his hands on her shoulders and kneading the tight muscles there.

"Perfect!"

"What's perfect?" he asked.

"Social media personas are easy to craft but hard to undo. We can use these"—she held up the book—"to our advantage."

Sara stiffened. "I'm not sure—"

"Be sure. Look, it's like this." Rebecca sat on the stool next to Sara's. "We need a distraction. The *team* needs a break from the media. So, we give them what they want. Access, carefully crafted, completely controlled on your terms, but access none-theless."

"And they'll just suddenly leave us alone?" Sara asked. "I find that hard to believe."

Mike did as well.

"Look, the issue is exposure. We don't have enough of the right kind. We haven't given a statement. Everyone is clamoring for the first shot at one. This gives you the chance to control the way it comes out."

Sara glanced back over her shoulder at him, raised her brows.

"This is your decision, Sara girl. They're your drawings, your life you'd share—"

"Well, technically, it's *our* life we'd share," she said, ice creeping into the edges of her tone.

He sighed. "You know what I mean. The exposure is going

to be worse for you. The Internet is way harder on women than men."

A roll of blue eyes. "That is true."

Rebecca began humming the *Jeopardy* theme. "Three hundred dollars an hour."

"What?" he asked.

"Three hundred dollars an hour is my going rate, but feel free to take your time."

"That's outrageous," Sara said.

"I'm good at my job."

Mike raised a brow. "I'd hope so."

"Don't talk to me, you overpaid rink rat."

Her insult was delivered with a smile and a wink, and he couldn't help but chuckle, especially when Sara giggled. "She does have a point."

"Of course I do." Rebecca stood and tapped her toe impatiently against the hardwood floor. "So, are you in?"

"Yes." Rebecca fist-pumped at Sara's answer. "Just tell me what you want me to do."

"I'll take care of everything," she said, already heading to the door, heels clicking, fingers typing on her cell. "You won't have to worry about a thing."

Why didn't Mike find her words reassuring?

THIRTY-ONE

Sara

THE GOLD WERE on their worst losing streak of the season. They dropped another game to Vancouver, making it six games in a row.

A few more losses, and their playoff hopes would be in jeopardy.

Sara knew this because it was on every sports news show.

Sara knew this because her poor influence was the lead story on every entertainment talk show.

She also knew this because of the fan in front of her.

She'd ventured out of Mike's house for the first time in ten days, wanting to see Mitch and needing to get out of her gilded prison.

The gallery was doing well, and Mitch had liked several of her drawings enough to display them. Which she considered the least she could do after creating the chaos at his store. Though, thankfully, not showing up for work meant the press had pretty much left.

She'd snuck through the back door, picked through the

crowded and disorganized storeroom, cringing all the while, and spent ten minutes in normality.

Then a customer had come in.

One who was also a Gold fan. Who'd recognized her.

And . . . cue awesomeness.

"You're fucking with the team, a goddamned distraction. Leave those boys alone." The man was middle-aged with a huge potbelly, but there was nothing soft about his expression. He stared at her, fury in his eyes, spittle spraying from his mouth as he raged.

Stepping back or cowering wasn't her first instinct. She'd been through this particular rodeo before. In fact, this was actually almost *calm*, based on some of the vitriol she'd dealt with after her medal had been taken away.

Usually ignoring was best, so she didn't know why she attempted to answer. Reasoning with people like this was pointless. But nevertheless, Sara opened her big, fat mouth and got an entire two words out before the man cut her off. "I'm not—"

"I'll tell you what you are. Worthless. A fucking cheater who likes to whore herself—"

"Stop. Right. There."

Mitch.

"Get out of my store."

She'd never heard that tone come from her boss's mouth. It was scary.

"Who the fuck are you?" The man spat—yes, literally spat—at Mitch.

"You have three seconds to leave or—"

"What?" The man gestured to Mitch's plum suit, the pristine striped tie. "You'll make me?" he sneered.

"In fact, I will."

"You fucking fa—" The homophobic slur didn't make it into the air.

"And that's enough, thank you." A huge man in a suit that was not nearly as nice as her boss's stepped from the back room, grabbed the man's arm, and escorted him to the door, which Mitch helpfully held open.

A second later, the pane of metal and glass was locked, and the man turned to face her.

"Supposed to be with you today," he said by way of explanation.

Mitch raised a brow in her direction.

She shrugged. "Apparently, I have a bodyguard."

"I'd say you need one."

She guessed she did.

Her sigh was loud, and he bumped her shoulder, smiling coaxingly at her. "Let's take a look at a few more of these, okay?"

They flipped through her book, and Mitch carefully cut a few drawings out in order to try different matting and frame options.

"This will do for now," he said after they'd spent another hour on the process. "I know this whole situation is screwed up, but it has done wonders for your production."

She laughed. "If there's a positive in the media tracking me like a dog, then it's that."

"Be safe, okay?" He raised a brow in the direction of the security guard standing in the corner, trying to be unobtrusive while being completely the opposite.

Six feet tall and wide as a Mack truck tended to be out of place in a gallery.

"Thanks, Mitch," she said, giving him a hug before crossing over to the man. "I'm Sara."

He glanced down at her outstretched hand and shook it as carefully as he might handle a fragile glass sculpture. "Pascal." A beat. "Perhaps you shouldn't sneak out next time?"

Remorse swept through her because she *had* snuck out. As

in, she had slipped through a gate in the back fence and called an Uber from two streets over. But she hadn't done it to avoid the security. She'd done it to evade the press.

"I'm an adult," she said, feeling guilty despite herself. "I don't exactly need a chaperone."

Mitch coughed, and she glared at him.

"Mr. Stewart asked that I keep you safe."

Nice of him to tell her that, she mentally complained, even though in the next heartbeat she knew she was being unfair.

Mike was out of town with the team, would continue to be so at regular intervals. He was trying to protect her from exactly the kind of asshole who'd confronted her in the store.

Holding on to that feeling, she wriggled her phone from her pocket and texted Mike.

I love you, Hot Shot.

He wouldn't get the message for a couple of hours since it was a practice day, but it was vitally important she send it anyway. Second chances didn't come around too often, and she needed, *needed* to not screw theirs up.

"Wake up, sleepyhead," Mike said the next morning.

Early the next morning.

Really, freaking, insanely, crazily early.

Sara rolled over and shoved her head under the pillow. "No."

She'd stayed up late the night before, waiting for Mike to get home, sketching into oblivion after watching the man from the gallery recite his encounter with her phrase-by-bitchy-phrase on the evening news. Never mind that she'd barely gotten two words out.

A story was a story, and hers at the moment was a front-page one. And so, Mr. Potbelly would be enjoying his fifteen minutes, and the local news station had an exclusive.

"Time to get up, sweetheart."

"It's too—" She screeched when the blanket was ripped from her body, and the freezing air hit her skin. "Mike!"

She was naked, of course. The pajamas they'd retrieved from her apartment had lasted all of five minutes.

"Up," he said and smacked her butt. Hard.

"You're an asshole!"

"And you're awake." A kiss to the base of her spine, big hands cupping her butt, kneading, rubbing what was no doubt a red-*ass* handprint on her right cheek.

Her hips canted up, and her temper waned. She sighed, thoroughly out of sleep's clutches now.

"Yes, I am—oh God!"

He'd slipped his fingers between her thighs then bent and flicked his tongue against her—

"Put these on."

A pair of sweats landed on the bed next to her, followed by a shirt. "I need fresh—" she said, starting to sit up.

Underwear smacked her in the face. A sports bra landed in her lap.

With a glare, she got dressed. "I'm afraid to mention socks."

Mike smirked and held up a hand. "I've got you covered." He knelt at her feet and tugged on a pair of patterned cotton crew socks then slipped on her sneakers.

"Anything else?"

"Yup." His fingers wrapped around her wrist, and he pulled her up from the bed.

"Good grief, what else could you possibly—?"

The rest of her words were muffled when he hauled a sweatshirt over her head. "That."

"Mike," she warned.

"You're supposed to be the morning person," he teased.

"Remind me of that when it's a reasonable time."

He chuckled, pushed her into the bathroom. "Brush your teeth."

"I should make you deal with my dragon breath," she muttered, snatching up her brush and putting her hair into a loose ponytail.

"Except you can't stand when your teeth are fuzzy."

She stilled, one hand on her toothbrush, the other on the toothpaste. Little details. He *always* remembered the little details. What type of pencil she liked to draw with. Her favorite ice cream. The way she took her coffee. That she hated kale but loved broccoli.

That she couldn't function without scrubbed teeth.

Why hadn't she accepted that damn ring? That perfect, wonderful promise of a future.

A future he hadn't brought up again over the last weeks. A future she desperately wanted. Because he was being patient. For *her*—a crazy, emotionally frazzled chick with a checkered past.

"You really don't care, do you?"

"About what?"

"My past."

He rolled his eyes, leaned back against the wall. "Now *that* question doesn't even deserve an answer."

This man.

Love spilling over the edges of her heart, she brushed and rinsed, and then with minty fresh breath, she walked over to Mike and kissed him.

Sara put everything she had into that kiss, every drop of

love, every bit of pain from the past, every ounce of guilt for refusing to do the right thing and step aside for the good of the team.

She gave it everything she had until her brain screamed for oxygen, and she had to pull back.

"Thank you," she murmured, eyes misty.

"For what?"

"For finding me again."

"Oh, Sara girl," he said, sounding a little choked up. "I shouldn't have let you go in the first place."

"It's not—"

He waved her off. "I shouldn't have brought that up. No more past talk, okay?" When she nodded, he snagged her hand. "Now, come on. I've got your coffee downstairs, and we don't want to be late for your surprise."

THIRTY-TWO

Mike

MIKE GAVE Pascal a fist-bump as he led a blindfolded Sara out the back gate. A car was parked on the street, not his, but a rental the security company had arranged for him.

He buckled Sara into the passenger seat and was driving away from the house just as the sky began to lighten.

It might be insanely early and way before the hour that he normally wanted to get up, but he was practically giddy with excitement.

He'd woken, showered, dressed, double-checked that every detail was in place, all before Sara had moved a muscle.

Though, in fairness to her, he had kept them both up very late into the night. He knew the attention was weighing on her, and though Rebecca was working on shifting the public image of Sara, it wasn't a fast process, especially when the team wasn't playing well.

When Pascal told him what had happened at the gallery—

Suffice it to say, he was glad he hadn't been there.

At least the bodyguard had handled things calmly. If *he'd*

seen some asshole come at Sara like that . . . Mike shook his head, knowing there was no way he would have been able to stop himself from punching the fucker.

"Not that I'm opposed to a blindfold in some cases," Sara said, finally speaking and sounding a lot more like her normally chipper early-morning self, "but are you going to tell me where we're going?"

He filed that bit of information—blindfolds could be used in a variety of manners—away for later use. "Nope."

"Umm. You remember that I don't like surprises, right?"

"From me, you do, remember?" When she sighed, he laughed. "And that's still a nope." He grinned at her, not that she could see it.

Before she could question him further, he turned on the radio or rather queued up his playlist.

If he was going full-out for a romantic sunrise surprise, he needed appropriately sappy music.

James Blunt's "You're Beautiful" filtered through the car's speakers.

Heaven help him if the guys ever got a hold of his phone.

But Sara's reaction was worth it.

She stilled, sniffed, and fumbled around until her hand was on his thigh. "Oh, Mike."

"Not too cheesy?" he teased.

"Perfect amount of Swiss," she said, lips twitching.

"Good," he said, taking one hand off the steering wheel and placing it over hers where it rested on the top of his thigh, dangerously close to his cock . . . which was supposed to be behaving.

Since it wasn't, he casually inched her hand a little lower.

Not slyly enough, apparently. Fingers slipped from his, crept up. "What's in your pants, Hot Shot?"

He snorted. "Pretty sure, you and he are on a first-name

basis, sweetheart. Now"—he slid her palm back down—"we're almost there. Behave."

"Where's *there*?"

"Nice try."

Mike waved at the guard and pulled through into the deserted parking lot. Or, *nearly* deserted since there was one other car.

Brit winked at him when he led Sara inside the arena and gave him a thumbs-up as they walked by.

"Why does it smell like disinfectant?"

"Because the crew is thorough."

"Did you bring me to a gym?" she asked.

"Not exactly." He pushed open the door to the arena, felt the rush of cool air hit his skin. "Though there is a gym here."

He slid the blindfold from her eyes.

Two pairs of skates rested on a black pad near the Zamboni door. Two folding chairs were beside them. The lights were dim, just enough to see the ice, but since the arena was technically closed, it was just the two of them out here.

Music, faint at first then growing louder, came over the speakers, and Mike smiled.

Brit was playing her role to a T and he realized he'd have to buy her and Stefan dinner, especially when he saw his captain slipping in behind Sara to set a basket and thermos near the chairs.

Sara didn't notice. Hell, *he* barely noticed because he was looking at Sara.

Watching the play of emotions over her face: fear, longing, pleasure, need, hesitation. Hers was a rolling reel of feelings, and he wondered which one she'd settle on.

Anger, perhaps, that he'd brought her in the first place. Relief that she might feel the ice beneath her feet.

Her eyes slid closed, and she inhaled.

"Mike," she said. "You're killing me."

"You're not mad?"

"Mad?" She shook her head. "I— Can I touch it?"

He didn't answer, just tugged her close to the edge of the open door, up to the strip of plastic that led onto the rink.

She bent, reached down, and touched the ice. Then promptly drew back. "It's cold!"

He laughed. "First time in an ice rink, is it?"

"Shut up." She flicked her fingers at him, spraying flecks of water in his direction. "I'd forgotten how it felt. How it can numb and burn all at once. The freeze permeating your layers of clothes, making you shiver, but that same cold then feeling so good at the end of a routine."

She stood and seemed to truly *see* the space around them for the first time.

Mike knew what she saw. Concrete stairs. Hints of gold fabric peeking out from the black-plastic bottoms of the folded seats. Blank screens around the edges and on the Jumbotron. Advertisements on the boards. A sheet of white broken up by red and blue in front of them.

"So this is your view, huh?"

"One of them," he said, touching her cheek. "Kind of prefer this one, though."

"Can I go on?"

"Well, *I'm* not wearing those pretty white skates."

She laughed. "No *The Cutting Edge* moment for us?"

"Not happening." He crossed to one of the chairs and patted the cushion next to him. "Come over here."

Together they slipped on their skates. Mike was faster only because Sara was having a moment with hers. She stroked the leather like it was the finest silk, touched the laces like they were made of woven gold, and checked the edge on the blade with keen eyes.

"They're sharp," he told her. "Billie—" the team's equipment manager "—took care of it for me."

"Does he even know how to sharpen figure skates?" she teased before consenting that the edges looked perfect and pushing her feet into the boots.

The laces were tightened and threaded around their grommets a few seconds later, and then she was on her feet, or rather, her skates.

"Ready?" he asked.

She nodded. "I can't believe you did this for me."

Her hand fit perfectly in his, two halves coming together to form a whole. It had always been that way. "I would do anything for you."

For a second, her eyes dimmed, but then she visibly shook herself. Straight shoulders, raised chin, smiling lips. "Ready for me to teach you a thing or two, Hot Shot?"

THIRTY-THREE

Sara

SARA PAUSED at the edge of the ice. She was being ridiculous, drawing the experience out when she could already be *doing* it.

But it had been ten years since she'd set foot on the ice—not counting that horrendous night with Leo.

And she wanted to savor the experience.

Breathing in that intrinsic rink scent . . . feeling the damp air in her lungs, the first crunch of ice beneath her feet . . .

"Please tell me that you're not having an orgasm over there without me."

Mike swept his thumb beneath her eyes, wiping away tears she hadn't realized were falling.

"Is it too much?" he asked.

"Honestly?" Her teeth found her lip. "Yes," hurrying to add when his face fell, "but in a good way. In the *best* way. I never thought I'd get this again, and you gave it to me."

"Well, it's not screaming crowds, but it *is* regulation size."

For the first time since her competing days, Sara stepped

onto the ice, and just as always, her smile locked into place. Not the fake one that hid pain, but the one that came from deep inside.

From doing something she loved.

From being with *someone* she loved.

"These are so light," she said, lifting a foot and gliding forward. She wasn't as steady as she'd once been, but, like riding a bike, it was coming back. "They must have cost a fortune."

"Skate technology has come a long way," he said. "You'll have to feel how light mine are."

Laughing, she glided away, turning at center ice and skating backward around the encircled Gold logo there.

Cross over. Cross over. Cross—

Whoa.

Throwing on the brakes, she looked sheepishly up at Mike who nodded encouragingly. "Slowly, honey. Take a few laps."

Nodding, she began running through what used to be her warm-up routine. Edge-work, balancing, crossovers, and then, without really thinking about it, she set up for a jump.

The move was a simple one, relatively speaking. A double-Salchow that was sloppy and totally under-rotated, but it felt fucking fantastic.

Applause echoed across the rink, and she glanced over at Mike.

He skated toward her, grabbed her hand, and tugged her against his chest. "Really? A double on your first time out?"

She snorted. "If you could call that ugly thing a double." But she was grinning, and it was almost as though her skates weren't even touching the ice.

"Gonna make it pretty?"

"Hell, yes, I am."

He tapped her butt. "Good, go on and show me what you've got."

Nodding, she skated over and set up the jump. Cool air slid along her scalp, ruffled her ponytail. She bent her leg, tensed every muscle in her body, brought her arms in, and . . .

Midway through the air, her back protested.

Sara compensated, instincts honed by years of competition, and managed to land the jump. The landing was definitely not the prettiest one she'd ever completed, but it was leaps and bounds better than that first attempt.

And she was done.

At least with the tricky stuff.

"You okay?" Mike was at her side in an instant.

"I'm good." In truth, she hadn't felt this exhilarated in years.

"Your back? I should have thought of—"

She jumped.

But this time instead of launching herself into the air, she hurled herself at Mike.

Who managed to catch her . . . or well, steady her, before falling to the ice himself.

Giggles burst out of her. "I'm so—sorry."

He was watching her with such an expression of outrage that she couldn't catch her breath because she was laughing too hard. "I-I would . . . have thought—big hockey guy like you—steadier on your skates."

"'Toepick,'" he said and grabbed her foot.

Instead of cracking her skull on the ice, Mike managed to manipulate her body midair so she landed on top of him, then wrapped his arms tight around her waist. "While you're down here," he murmured.

"Wh—?"

He kissed her.

There were almost too many sensations to process. The cold radiating up from the ice, the heat of Mike's body, his lips soft against hers. Her clothes felt too tight and she wanted them off, wanted him on her, *in* her.

"I can't believe you *toepicked* me," she said, heart pounding, when they finally broke away for air. The line was from *The Cutting Edge*, the scene when the hockey player was trying to learn how to use figure skates . . . and not succeeding because he kept tripping over the set of spikes at the front of the blades that hockey skates didn't have.

"Too tempting to resist," he told her. "Especially with you smirking after checking me to the ice."

"It wasn't a check!"

One brown brow rose.

"I wanted to kiss you, okay?" Her tone was begrudging. "For being so nice."

He chuckled, amusement all over his expression. "Nice? No." He pushed his elbows under him and helped her up to her skates then waggled his eyebrows. "Don't you know that I'm a bad boy?"

"I know that you're ridiculous."

"You love me."

Her heart clenched. "I do," she murmured. "I do love you."

"So," he said, and she noticed that he shifted, one knee on the ice, as though he was ready to stand up.

But instead of rising, he continued to kneel in front of her.

And then he reached into his pocket.

Her breath caught when he pulled out a box.

Covered in blue velvet, it fit easily into the palm of his hand. She inanely noticed that and a dozen other details: the maniacal eyes of the Gold logo behind him as he knelt at center ice, Brit standing at the Zamboni door, phone held up in the air, spotlights shining down on them, the random car dealership advertisement on the boards . . . and the look in Mike's eyes.

"I love you, Sara. Always have, always will. I know I'm not the greatest with romantic gestures—"

She snorted. Which was so *not* her fault, the big liar.

Laughter came from Brit's end of the ice. Mike flicked a gaze over his shoulder and shook his head. "The women in my life—"

"Make it so much better," she finished.

Now a male thread joined Brit's giggles.

"True," Mike said, grinning. "Okay, so maybe I've got the romance bit down, but without you, my life doesn't mean a damn thing, Jumping Bean."

"Aw . . ." Brit again.

He rolled his eyes. "I'm sorry for the crowd. Brit said you might want a video of this, but really, she's just nosy."

"You're just realizing that?" Stefan called. "Pull the trigger already, Stewie! We know she's going to say yes!"

Mike glanced at her nervously. "You are going to say yes, aren't you?"

Stefan and Brit were joined by more of the team, who catcalled.

God, she loved this man . . . and his friends.

"Mike," she murmured

"Oh, fuck," he said, opening the box and displaying a gorgeous princess-cut diamond in a platinum setting. "Please say you'll marry me, Sara girl."

Sara paused just long enough to make him sweat, but not long enough to be cruel. She did love him, after all.

"I was just going to say your original choice for a ring was perfect."

He burst to his feet and yanked her close. "I love you so fucking much."

Then he was kissing her, and the team was cheering, and he was slipping the ring on her finger.

"I'll put the other one on later," he promised. "For now, I just need to see you with a ring."

She touched her lips to his. "That I can live with."

Someone whooped, and she inclined her head toward the team. "Should we go face the crowd?"

"If we have to."

"You have to!" Brit yelled. "I need to see that diamond!"

THIRTY-FOUR

Mike

EMERALDS AGAINST PALE SKIN.

Mike nuzzled Sara's neck and played with the ring sitting on her finger. It glittered in the sunlight.

She was dead asleep, something he was responsible for. But he was playing eight games in ten days, both at home and on the road, and wouldn't be seeing much of her, so he'd needed to make the most of their time.

Between travel and pre-game routines, plus normal practices and training, he would be living and breathing hockey for the next while.

Not that he minded. Or not normally anyway.

He did worry about leaving her alone so much.

Though Spence had delivered a message from Monique—basically a promise to watch out for Sara while he and the team were otherwise occupied.

And Rebecca had scheduled time with Sara the next day. A progress update on the social media stuff and more *plans*.

But it had been several weeks since the story of their relationship broke, and the press still sat outside his gate. Frankly, it was making him a little crazy. He couldn't go on his patio, have his blinds open without feeling as though eyes were on him.

He guessed they were . . . but knowing that still made his skin crawl.

If only the team could link a few wins together, get the focus back on hockey and away from drama—

"Why are you staring at me?" Sara asked, voice and hair sleep-mussed.

"Because you're beautiful," he said, pushing back the strands to kiss her jaw.

She grunted.

"You used to be a morning person."

"You used to not keep me up to the wee hours of the night."

That was true. But by the time he'd gotten home from the previous night's game, it had been after midnight.

Pascal had already driven Sara home from the arena—they'd found it tended to create less commotion if they drove separately—and she had been asleep before he walked into the bedroom.

"You were naked."

Her face was in the mattress, slightly muffling her words, but he saw her smile, or at least the crease in her cheeks as her lips turned up.

"When do you leave?"

"Couple hours." He kissed one shoulder, then the other, loved that her breathing hitched. "What do you have planned?"

"Monique invited me over for dinner and to watch the game." She rolled onto her back. "Do you think it's safe? I mean, I don't want to stir up anything, not with Mirabel in the crosshairs."

"Pascal will keep you all safe. I have no doubt about that." He twined a piece of her hair around his finger, reveled in how soft it was. "But it would probably be best if you don't go out too much."

"Yeah," she said before making a visible effort to lighten her tone. "Plus is, I've got more money than I know what to do with. Mitch has sold everything I gave him, and he needs more already. Pretty soon, I'll be flush enough to get my own place." Her hands spread, framing an imaginary house. "My own little castle on the hill. I think I'll put in a moat, with alligators . . . except they'll only eat paparazzi."

"Except, you'll stay here," Mike said, bristling, though he knew she was joking.

He wanted Sara to be happy, and if that meant art, then certainly to be successful at that, but he also wanted her in his home, his room, his bed.

She giggled. "Sorry. When Mitch said you'd get all growly and caveman, I should have believed him." A soft palm cupped his cheek. "Thought I made it clear that there was no place I'd rather be."

The security company had moved everything out of Sara's apartment, not that she had much, and she'd prepaid with her art earnings for the penalty to get out of her lease.

Last night she'd offered to pay him rent.

Rent! The other half of his soul wanted to pay for the privilege of staying with him. He should be paying her, for fuck's sake, not the other way around.

Sara was everything . . . and frustratingly independent.

The woman hadn't even let him help with closing down her apartment or getting the drawings to Mitch. She wouldn't let him cook for her on meal days or pick up anything heavier than the TV remote.

Hell, he was surprised he was allowed to have sex.

That would probably go next. Couldn't risk overtaxing his muscles, now could he?

"What are you thinking?" she asked. "Your face went all scowly."

"Rent." One word, a shake of his head, and Sara understood the context exactly.

She rolled her eyes. "What kind of person would I be if I didn't offer?"

"Normal."

A huff as she clambered into his lap. The sheets pooled around their hips, and his cock hardened at the sight of her breasts just inches from his face.

"Really?" Her tone was droll, but her body gave her away. She arched against him, rubbing her wetness along his erection. "Again?"

"You're naked." He nipped at her neck. "And wet."

"There is that."

In one swift movement, he flipped them and pinned her hips to the bed. "I'm leaving in a couple of hours."

A flash of white teeth. "There is that too."

"I'm hard."

Fingers wrapped around his length as she guided him home. "That you are. Now"—she leaned up, whispered in his ear —"show me what you can do with that."

He grinned then proceeded to demonstrate his abilities.

Twice.

LATER, seated next to Blane on the team's jet, he stared at the text from Sara.

Fewer camera goons today. Maybe we're finally old news.

That was the best thing he'd heard, aside from her moans that morning.

He sent a heart emoji, not thinking twice until Blane glanced over Mike's shoulder and shook his head.

"Whipped, dude," his teammate muttered. "Fucking emojis. Might as well turn in your man card."

"Don't even care, B. I've got Sara, so I'll take as much flack as you can dish out about being pussy-whipped." He shook his head, knowing he was grinning like an idiot and not giving a damn.

Max, who was in the row in front of them, turned around and said, "Let's talk about your playlist—"

"Not today, boys," Brit called from a few seats back. She was cozied up to Stefan. Must be nice. "Mike knows his romance. You should be taking notes, not giving him shit."

"But I like giving it to Mi—"

"Finish that fucking sentence, and you die," Mike gritted out.

Max chuckled but turned around and flopped back down into his seat, iPad already at the ready, figurines spilling into the space next to him.

Mike glanced at Blane, who was almost preternaturally still. "You good?"

A flash of pain crossed his face, the same hurt that always seemed on the periphery of his expression whenever he saw Brit with Stefan. The man held a flame for Brit, and while she loved him—they'd grown up playing together—it had never been more than a sister's love.

Fuck, he sounded like Oprah.

Blane's face cleared. "Yup. Just thinking about the next game. We've got to get more traffic in front of the net if we're going to score. Their goaltending is too strong otherwise."

They chatted for a few minutes about the upcoming games

and the adjustments Coach wanted them to make, both defensively and offensively, then each plugged in their headphones and tuned out for the rest of the hour-long flight.

When they landed, Blane slipped off the plane ahead of the rest of them.

THIRTY-FIVE

Sara

SARA AND PASCAL pulled up to Monique's house about thirty minutes before puck drop. It had taken forever to shake their tail, but she hadn't wanted to lead the paparazzi to Spence and Monique's home.

None of them needed *that* chaos.

The house was quaint, in an older part of the city, but nicely kept up. It had Victorian details—ornate trim, a pitched roof, was painted in a deep green with bright white accents, and was boxed in by a neat, flower-filled yard.

The sight was homey, and with the sun drifting toward the horizon, she pulled out her phone and snapped a few pictures. She'd have to ask Monique if she could draw it.

"I'll be around," Pascal said after she'd stowed her cell. "Text if you need anything." And then he disappeared into the shadows.

Literally walked into the darkness and vanished from view.

"That's super creepy."

His soft laugh trailed her up to the door.

She hesitated before pressing the bell, suddenly nervous. Like she was a teenager on a date for the first time and—

The knob turned, the panel swung open, and Mirabel wrapped her arms tight around her waist.

"Wow," the girl said. "I forgot how little you are." Small hands measured their heights, passing from the top of her head to Sara's shoulder. Yes, pathetically, the seven-year-old was almost as big as she.

"You're tall for your age," Monique said. "Comes from having a giraffe of a mother and a hockey-player dad."

Mirabel nodded vigorously. "My dad is sixty-six."

Sara grinned. "Wow, he looks good for his age."

"Come in. Come in," Monique said. "Six feet six isn't anything too special amongst athletes, but add in my crazy genes —" She patted her hips, gesturing to the ridiculously long legs holding her up.

"You're beautiful," Sara said, following them into the house. "I always wanted to be taller."

"We're all beautiful in our own ways," Mirabel said.

"That's right," Monique replied, ruffling her hair. "Why don't you go wash up? Dinner's almost ready."

"Can I show Sara my room first?"

Monique's eyes flicked over to Sara's. She shrugged. Looking at little girls' rooms wasn't something she was in the habit of, but if Mirabel wanted to show her . . .

"Okay."

"Yay! Come on!" She grabbed Sara's hand and started dragging her down the hall.

"Slowly!" Monique called. "Show her *slowly*."

Mirabel's feet decreased their speed. Slightly.

Sara was led past two closed doors and through an open one into a . . . pink-splosion.

Pink carpet. Pink walls. Pink curtains and bed coverings.

The only thing that wasn't pink was the sparkling silver rhinestones bedazzling the edge of *everything*.

"Do you like it?"

She blinked, eyes trying to adjust to the visual onslaught. "It's very pretty."

"I love pink!" Mirabel yelled, jumping in a circle and doing a little dance in the middle of her fuchsia area rug.

"I can tell," Sara deadpanned, walking toward a collection of stuffed animals. The only non-pink toy in the whole place was a plush Gold skater. It wore a face-mask, goalie pads, and a jersey with . . . Brit's number?

"Don't tell Dad," Mirabel whispered. "But Brit's my favorite Gold player."

Sara laughed loudly. "You're the best, kiddo."

"I know." Mirabel bent to pull a book off her shelf. It had— no surprise—a pink cover.

"Oh yeah?" Sara took the book when Mirabel pressed it into her hand.

"That's what my dad says." A pause. "You can call me Mira," she said. "All my friends do."

She tugged one of Mirabel's—Mira's—curls. "Thanks, Mira. You can call me . . . Sara." When the little girl giggled, she shrugged. "My name is pretty short already."

"True." Mira opened the book, turning pages until she stopped on a chapter. "Can you read this to me?"

Sara smiled. "Just so happens that I love to read."

"Me too!"

She read aloud to Mira until someone cleared her throat from the doorway. Turning her head, she saw Monique watching them, a relaxed smile on her face. "Dinner's ready, and the boys are almost on TV. Wash up, sweetheart."

"Okay!" Mira jumped to her feet and grabbed the Gold plush then sprinted out the door and into the bathroom across the hall. Sara blinked as the door slammed closed, followed seconds later by the toilet flushing, bottles clattering, water splashing, and finally the door was wrenched back open as Mira skidded out and ran down the hall.

The girl appeared to only have one speed.

"Did I keep her too long?" Sara asked.

Monique was studying her, expression unfathomable.

It cleared at her question. "No. She would have gladly kept you here reading to her until she, or you, passed out from exhaustion." A hesitation. "I'm just trying to figure you out."

Sara laughed uncomfortably. "I'm not too complicated."

Monique shook her head. "Exceptionally talented. Nice. Gorgeous. How did you get mixed up in that scandal? No," she added when Sara sucked in a breath. "Don't answer that. It was more rhetorical than anything. You just seem *so* nice."

"Nice people do bad things," Sara said softly, slipping a bookmark into Mira's book and setting it on the bed.

"That is one version of the truth." Monique's eyes narrowed. "But not yours, is it?"

"No."

"You know, in my modeling days, I met quite a few interesting people."

"Yeah?" Sara fussed with the hem of her shirt, pulling it down, smoothing out a few non-existent wrinkles.

"Yeah. One of those is an expert at private investigation. I can make a call, get you in touch—"

The knot in Sara's stomach loosened. "Thank you," she said. "But I think I'd like to try and keep the past where it belongs."

A beat of quiet passed, then Monique murmured a soft, "I understand." She tilted her head toward the hall, voice raising and growing decidedly chipper. "Now let's go eat. Spence has the start tonight, and I want to watch my man skate."

"Brit's not playing?" Mira asked as she ran back toward them. "Aw, man!"

"Don't tell her father she said that, okay?" Monique said, though her eyes were filled with laughter.

"Deal." She took a breath, wanting to force out the tension that had invaded from the seriousness of the last few moments. "Does Spence know that Brit is her favorite?" She nodded at the plush toy that Mira held.

"Oh yeah."

Sara and Monique both burst into giggles. They were still laughing when they sat down with bowls of rice, chicken, and veggies at the coffee table in front of the TV.

"It's not fancy," Monique said, passing her a fork and napkin, "but it's kind of a tradition."

"I think it's perfect."

As was the rest of the night. Mira cheered for the team between bites of food, coaxed Sara to read a few more chapters during intermission—a clear ploy to get out of doing the dishes that both she and her mom knew and ignored—and conked out halfway through the second period.

At intermission, Monique carried her daughter to her room while Sara washed up the rest of the plates and stacked them in the dishwasher.

"You're not driving, right?"

"No, Pascal is." She frowned. Out of sight, out of mind. She'd forgotten about the bodyguard hiding in the shadows. "He's around . . . somewhere."

"The security guy?"

Sara nodded. "He's really good at his job." Her lips twitched. "Almost too—"

"Good," Monique finished with her. "Yeah, I'm friends with the wife of his normal client."

"You're friends with *Devon Scott's* wife?" she asked then winced, because the question had almost been a shriek.

Monique smirked. "Yes. Becca is super cool."

Sara's cheeks went scorching hot. "Sorry, I'm a little star-struck. Mike mentioned that he used to play for the team, but he's just . . ." She rolled her eyes at herself. "I know I'm being ridiculous and yet those abs—"

"Gorgeous," Monique agreed. "One perk of being a hockey wife is the hot scenery."

They both broke down into giggles again.

When they finally got themselves under control, Monique asked, "How about a glass of wine?"

"Wine is everything," Sara said.

"Dork." Monique pulled out a corkscrew and a bottle of chardonnay.

A shrug. "That's a true story."

Laughing, she nodded at the screen. "Go on and sit. Your guy is on TV. Better enjoy him."

"You too," Sara teased. "*Your* guy is playing his ass off."

"Brit needed the break with so many games on the schedule. She'll be back on it tomorrow." Monique shrugged and poured two glasses. "Such is the life of a backup. Always the bridesmaid."

"Is it really bad?" Sara took the wine over to the coffee table.

"No. I mean, he wants to play, but he also knows his role for the team. His is as important as anyone's."

Sara nodded. Sometimes it wasn't the most well-known player who made the biggest difference.

"Just like I know where to hide my brownie stash so that little—and big—fingers won't find them." Monique held up a plate filled with gooey black squares.

Sara lifted her wine glass in a toast. "You're a genius."

"Hell yeah, I am," Monique said, shoving a brownie in her mouth and setting the plate on the table.

There might have only been eight minutes left in the period, but she and Monique still managed to pack away that plate of chocolate as well as the entire bottle of wine. And when the game ended—in an overtime win, yes!—they were pleasantly tipsy.

"Let's do this again, sometime," Monique said, hugging Sara. Her caramel cheeks held the slightest flush, and her breath smelled like wine.

Not that Sara was in any better state. Her face was hot, probably red as a tomato, and her head was pleasantly muddled. Wine was good for her stress. Look at that.

"Definitely," she said, squeezing back and turning toward the car.

Oh, crap. She should have called Pascal.

Except that he materialized out of thin air, making the two of them squeak with shock. "Stop doing that," she said.

His lips twitched as he stepped into the light of the porch. "'I'm very, very sneaky.'"

Sara tilted her head to the side, studying him. "Did you really just quote an Adam Sandler movie to me?"

He didn't answer, just turned to Monique and said, "Lock up. I'll escort Ms. Jetty home."

Monique dipped to lock eyes with Sara and said, mock whisper, "He did quote Adam Sandler."

"I knew it! The line was from—"

"*Mr. Deeds.*"

"Terrible movie," Sara said.

"Horrible," agreed Monique. "But I still loved it."

"Me too!"

And cue more giggles. With a sigh, Pascal gently pushed

Monique back across the threshold and closed the front door. "Lock up," he said loudly.

The deadbolt slid into place. "Movie marathon. Your house. Thursday." Her voice was muffled.

"Deal," Sara said, talking with enough volume to be heard through the wood. "But what about Mira?"

She could always bring her.

"She gave you the go-ahead for the nickname? Dang girl. I don't even have that right."

They both snickered, and Pascal cleared his throat. With emphasis.

"Mirabel is at her grandma's that night."

"Then it's a date."

"Great," muttered Pascal.

"Night, Sara!"

"Night," she called and turned for the car.

Pascal beat her there, opening the door and making sure she was buckled in before he closed it. They were almost home before she came out of her pleasant, muddled, wine-chocolate fog to say, "Thank you. For bringing me."

He shrugged. "It's nothing."

"Except it's something to me."

His eyes flicked to hers for a second then back to the road. "I understand." A pause. "And I'm happy you have a friend."

They drove the rest of the way home in silence. They slid through the gate almost unobstructed—definitely less paparazzi —and he walked her to the door, making her wait in the entry while he did a sweep of the house.

Once he'd gone, she changed into her pajamas and fell into bed.

It felt like only seconds had passed before hands were shaking her awake. "Mike?" she asked, bleary-eyed.

"No," a female voice said. "I'm not Mike."

THIRTY-SIX

Mike

FINALLY, the Gold had won two games in a row. Mike and the rest of the team breathed a sigh of relief. They'd been ahead by a goal early in the game, but had given up the lead late in the second.

That second period had been a clusterfuck of epic proportions. The only good part had been the team rebounding.

First Blue had tied the game, and then Blane had gotten the overtime winner.

And finally, they were back on track again.

He sent a text to Sara, an ooey, gooey message that the guys would give him crap for. She wouldn't get it until the morning, but he wanted the first thing she saw when she woke up to be him. Or, well, his thoughts of her.

Whipped, and he didn't give a damn.

Slipping on his suit jacket, he followed Brit and Stefan out of the locker room and through the maze-like hallways beneath the arena. They stepped out into the parking lot and boarded the bus, the drone from the paparazzi basically nonexistent here in Southern California.

The celebrities watching the game had been way more interesting than mere athletes.

Plus, Sara was at home and not the arena, so the buzz around the team had dropped significantly.

Which was the singular good thing about being away from her.

Maybe the lack of a photo op would make for more peace when he got back.

The drive to the hotel in Anaheim was just over an hour, where their next game was, and he all but collapsed into his bed. He almost preferred the old days of roommates, compared to the empty hotel room without Sara.

Then he remembered how loudly Blane snored.

Empty was definitely better.

He tossed his suit over a chair to deal with in the morning and collapsed into the king-size bed.

And even though he missed Sara with a palpable ache, exhaustion dragged him under almost the moment his head hit the pillow.

MIKE WAS SO DEEPLY asleep that it took him a bit to realize the pounding was someone knocking at his door.

He rolled out of bed, wincing at the bright red numbers on the clock.

Five past five.

The knocking started again, and he hurried to the peephole. Coach was on the other side.

And Mike was in his underwear. Great.

Well, nothing to be done about it. He opened the door.

Coach Bernard's eyes were wild. "Coach, what's wrong?"

"Pants and shirt on. Grab your stuff. You need to go."

Mike moved, grabbing his slacks and undershirt off the chair, stuffing the rest of his suit into his bag. Fuck wrinkles.

"What is it?"

"A plane is waiting," Coach said, pulling open the door. "Normal circumstances don't apply to this."

It had to be Sara. Mike knew that. The knot in his gut knew, the ice pouring through his veins knew.

"Is she—?"

Devon Scott came around the corner then. "Come on, Stewart. Let's move. I'll explain on the way."

His former teammate didn't lead Mike to the elevator, instead pushed through the stairwell and pounded down the stairs. The lobby was quiet as they sped through to a waiting car. Once inside, he whipped toward Devon.

"What the fuck is going on?"

"Sara is . . ."

THIRTY-SEVEN

Sara

SO MUCH FOR her gilded prison.

Turned out all the security in the world didn't mean much when a person disregarded the law.

"You're trespassing," Sara murmured.

The woman who stood at the end of the bed looked crazy. Her ratty blond hair was yanked into a haphazard ponytail, thick black liner was smudged around her eyes, her clothes were stained and torn.

"Get up."

Not happening. Sara reached for her phone. Pascal had put his number on speed dial. She just needed to—

"Stop." The order was accompanied by a gun pointed in her direction.

Sara froze.

The woman smiled, revealing as many missing teeth as some of the guys on the Gold. "Ah, so you aren't *entirely* stupid. Now get up."

Sara slipped from the bed.

"Put on shoes."

She put on her shoes.

"Walk downstairs."

It wasn't like Sara could disobey, not with a gun pointed at her back.

"What do you want from me?" she asked as they descended. Could she delay long enough to get help? There was supposed to be a guard on duty at all times.

"I don't want anything from *you*," the woman snapped. "Freeze," she ordered when Sara headed for the front door. "Not there. Do I look stupid? Go out the back, away from the cameras."

"Where is Pascal?" she asked, stepping onto the back deck.

"You mean the Rico Suave wannabe? He served his purpose." The gun poked into Sara's spine, nudging her toward the stairs leading down to the yard.

Oh shit. Her throat went tight. If Pascal been hurt because of her . . .

Eyes burning, she turned to face the woman. "Why are you doing this?"

"Boo-hoo-hoo," the woman sneered. "Move it. This isn't about you or your tears. I got what I needed from you years ago. Now I need the same from Mike."

Sara hesitated at the top of the stairs then screamed when the gun went off.

Glass exploded around her as the window near her head shattered. "I said move!"

"O-okay." She hurried down the wooden stairs, stumbling when the woman shoved the barrel of the gun into her back again. The metal was hot, burning her skin through the thin cotton of her tank top.

"You always were a stupid bitch. Too dumb to see the

connection back then, too dumb to understand it now." Another shove, another moment of just catching her balance.

"To the back," the woman ordered when Sara hesitated at the bottom of the deck.

She turned for the garden gate. "Where are we going?"

"Somewhere to get Mike's attention."

"What?" Sara paused then winced when the gun shoved into her spine again. "B-but why do you need Mike's attention?"

"Because my son won't give me any *money*, you dumb whore!"

Sara gaped then whispered, "Your *son?*"

"My deadbeat of a son has cut me off!" Mike's mother, Patricia screamed. "Now you're going to—"

"You're not taking her anywhere."

The sun was still tucked behind the horizon, orange and red streaks just starting to lighten up the sky.

But she would recognize that voice even in the pitch black.

Pascal.

He stepped toward them, a gun in his hand. Sara had never thought that guns were a big deal. But having one prodding into her back, being sandwiched between two, either of which could easily end her life. . . and her cavalier attitude disappeared.

Patricia spat in Pascal's direction. "Didn't I already rough you up enough? Or maybe I need to hurt little Sara girl." With her free hand, she yanked Sara's hair hard, wrenching her neck and back and making her cry out. "Step the fuck away and let us by."

"Okay." Pascal moved back, tucking the gun away, and putting his palms up. "You don't need to hurt her."

"*Move.*" This order was to Sara and she stumbled forward, her spine on fire, her hip and scalp burning. When, she slipped past Pascal, she saw he had a huge dripping gash above one eye and was favoring one leg. *Oh God.* He was hurt, because of her. "She's got a gu—"

Pascal's eyes met hers for a brief moment before he lunged.

Sara would have been free if Mike's mother hadn't held tight to her ponytail. But her hair was still in Patricia's grip and so Pascal's leap knocked all three of them to the ground.

Pain lit up through her body. Every inch was on fire. The muscles in her back spasmed and lights flashed behind her eyes when her skull cracked against the ground. But Pascal was hurt, and they were scuffling and—

The gun went off again.

She almost didn't feel it. Then a burn bloomed up from the left side of her body.

"Sara?" Pascal's voice was near. And frantic.

"Here," she said inanely. "You good?"

"Hold on." Rustling was accompanied by pressure on her side. It was agony.

She screamed, apologized for the loud noise, knowing distantly that she shouldn't create a scene and draw in the paparazzi.

Pascal's voice rattled around the air, multiplying, overwhelming her senses. Ten Pascals were talking. Maybe more.

Lights. Noise. Pain.

Then black.

The black was welcome.

THIRTY-EIGHT

Mike

". . .BREAKING NEWS. Former skating champion, Sara Jetty, has been rushed to the hospital with a possible gunshot wound. The incident occurred on the property belonging to Mike Stewart, her boyfriend and current Gold player, in full view of several camera crews," the anchor said. "We've edited some of the footage about to play, but be warned this may be disturbing to some."

The television cut away from the newscaster in a prim suit jacket to the footage.

Mike wanted to look away from the iPad Devon held in front of them, but he couldn't, not when it was about Sara.

He watched a light turn on in the house then two figures come out onto his back deck—the crew must have positioned themselves near the garden gate. The video was slightly grainy then the film went into full focus.

"Fuck."

Sara was being prodded in the back with a gun . . . held by his mother.

Devon clicked up the volume. The words the women exchanged were faint but audible.

". . . too dumb to see the connection back then . . ."

His gaze collided with Devon's, who said, "I'll find out."

A gunshot rang out, then a scream and shattering glass. Sara was shuffled forward, his *fucking* mother the assailant.

And the world got another layer of why-in-the-ever-loving-fuck. *This* is why he'd left Sara alone a decade ago. Because his mother was insane, because his mother was so fucking far gone that she might have hurt the woman he loved.

And apparently Mike had been right to worry.

Pascal appeared in the frame, and there was a scuffle, another shot, and then the camera was bobbing, its shot frenzied as it ran toward the trio. Someone off camera was calling 9-1-1, another helped Pascal restrain his mother so he could move to Sara and begin working on her.

"We'll stop the footage there," the anchorwoman said. "Ms. Jetty is currently in critical condition at UCSF Medical Center."

Mike's phone buzzed. None of the flight attendants on the private jet had bothered to tell him or Devon to turn them off. Not with everything that was happening. He glanced at the screen and saw it was Brit wanting to know if Sara was okay.

He wished he knew.

Clicking it off, he glanced at the row of TVs mounted on the plane's wall. Several channels broadcasted the morning news, each breaking down what had happened to Sara overnight.

"Fuck," he said again, standing and shoving his hands into his hair. He gripped the back of his neck and paced the aisle, panic in every single cell.

A plane ride was the fastest way home. He got that. He just needed to be there already.

"She's alive, man," Devon said. "And Monique is by her side. Rebecca too."

"I shouldn't have left her."

"You couldn't—"

"Did you not see that the woman who shot her was my *mother*? Fuck, I can't even begin to describe the levels of how fucked up my life is. The person who delivered me into this world tried to kill the person I love the most."

"It's not your mother. It's the drugs."

Mike froze then dropped his head.

Devon knew all about a parent battling addiction. His father had been hooked on OxyContin, but *his* father also hadn't tried to kill anyone.

"That's not a fucking excuse!" he yelled at the floor, wrenching a hand through his hair, practically yanking it from his scalp. "My *mother* did it. *She* released the pictures, hurt Sara, and—"

Fuck. His voice broke. His knees gave out.

He buried his face in his hands, totally not giving a shit that tears were leaking between his fingers.

Devon placed a hand on his shoulder, squeezed hard. "You're right. The only person my dad hurt was himself, physically anyway. I'm sorry." A pause. "I thought Pascal would be— Well, I don't know how your mother got the jump on him."

Mike blew out a shuddering breath, lifted his head. "He was bleeding."

"Yeah, he was."

"It wasn't Pascal's fault." He stood with shaking legs, walked to the couch, and sank down.

Devon didn't respond. Rather, he was looking at his phone. "Update from Rebecca. They're taking Sara into surgery."

The flight attendant who had been standing—hiding—in the

galley came out. "If you could buckle in, the captain has just informed me that we'll be landing soon."

He nodded and clicked his seatbelt, but his mind was on Devon's words.

Surgery.

What if he didn't get the chance to say good-bye?

THIRTY-NINE

Sara

SARA'S EYES were glued shut. That was the only explanation. She couldn't lift her lids a millimeter, let alone open them completely.

Her side burned with a throbbing pain. Her nose was crusted. Her throat dry as a desert.

And there was a warm hand in hers.

The faintest hint of aftershave.

The scent permeated through the air, filled her nostrils, steadied her heart, and the pain dimmed.

Mike was there.

Drawing on her reserve of strength, she wrenched back her eyelids.

He was crammed into a wooden chair, half curled in on himself as he leaned over the bed, his head resting near her uninjured side, his hand gripping hers.

The door squeaked, and a woman in maroon scrubs poked her head in. When she saw Sara awake, she smiled and murmured that she would get the doctor.

Bits and pieces of what had happened began lining up in Sara's mind.

The woman, with a face that was sort of familiar. Mike's mother. The gun. Pascal.

Was Pascal okay?

She looked around as though the hospital room would somehow give her a clue to his well-being. There was nothing except a few food containers and paper coffee cups.

Her eyes drifted to the TV. It was on, showing the Gold were playing against the Ducks.

Why was Mike here when his team was on the ice?

Though—she squinted to read the score in the upper left corner of the screen—they were destroying the Ducks, eight to nothing. She watched the game wind down, the guys kicking butt and Brit making a number of good saves to lock in that shut-out.

When the buzzer rang, the team skated off the ice. Brit was given a pair of headphones, and the announcers began congratulating her on the win. Then they asked a question that wiped the smile off her face.

"How difficult was it to focus with what happened to Sara Jetty today?"

Brit shoved a piece of hair out of her face. "I'll be frank, Jim. It was rough. The team loves Sara. She's part of our family, and it was hard to focus on playing, knowing my friend was in surgery."

Sara's eyes clouded with tears.

"We got an update that she was out of the operating room and in recovery just before puck drop."

"That's the best news I've heard all year." Brit looked into the camera and said, "Sara, if you're watching, know we're thinking about you. Love you, girl."

They asked a few more questions about the game, but Sara barely heard them.

The difference between her previous injury and this one, between her former and current lives, was almost laughable.

"I am so lucky," she murmured.

Mike started, blinking as he lifted his head. But before he could say anything, another voice chimed in. "Yes, you are."

Sara glanced at the door, where the doctor had apparently slipped into her room. He wore blue scrubs and still had booties over his shoes. "I'm Dr. Clark. I did your surgery. Sorry for the delay, I was assisting with a colleague's procedure, but I wanted to see you right away." He crossed over to her and slid the blankets down then lifted her gown enough to see her side. She was bandaged so the incision wasn't visible—a fact Sara was grateful for—but he gently palpated her abdomen. "Good," he eventually said, fixing her gown and the blankets.

"What happened?"

"You were shot."

Her snort hurt. "That much I surmised. I had surgery?"

Dr. Clarks' lips twitched. "They don't call me a surgeon for nothing. But in all seriousness, the bullet was nearly a through and through. The ER thought you were in the clear. Then they realized your spleen had been nicked."

Her spleen? That sounded serious. She didn't even know what the organ did, but it sounded important.

"I was able to repair the nick, but we'll need to watch it. Make sure it takes."

"Why doesn't that make me feel any better?"

He laughed. "Because it's a serious injury. You also had a blood transfusion and will be on IV antibiotics for a few days." Dr. Clark squeezed her hand before picking up an iPad and updating something on it. "The nurse will check in soon. But if the pain gets to be too much, you're attached to a morphine pump. Just push that red button."

A minute later, he was gone, and she and Mike—who hadn't said a word—were alone.

She turned to him, opened her mouth—

"I need to go," he said, pushing to his feet and striding out the door.

"Mi—"

He left, and she couldn't chase after him.

MIKE WAS a ghost over the next few days, disappearing when she showed any sign of being awake.

Sara knew because she'd tested her theory.

She'd watched him through slit lids sit next to her on the bed, but the moment she moved or opened her eyes, he was up and out of the room. Ostensibly, he was off to get her a glass of ice or another blanket, but she was onto him.

He didn't want to be with her.

If she was another woman, she might have thought he wanted to dump her. But she was Sara, and he was Mike, and they were like peanut butter and jelly, bananas and chocolate, French fries and ketchup.

They were meant to be together, and she wasn't going to let them fall apart.

Mike came back into the room, blanket in hand, and glanced around like he'd expected to have been gone long enough that she'd fallen back asleep.

That tactic might have worked the previous few days, but she was recovering nicely. Dr. Clark said he would discharge her the following afternoon if everything continued to look good.

So today she was awake more than asleep. And Mike wasn't going to avoid her.

Fate, apparently, had other plans.

The moment he'd sat down in the chair, Rebecca knocked on the door.

"Hey, Sara. You feel up to chatting?"

"I—"

Mike whack-a-moled out of his seat. "I'll leave you two alone to talk."

Slippery little sucker.

Rebecca frowned. "He okay?"

Sara shook her head. "No. I think he feels guilty. Not that he'll talk to me about it."

"Men." Rebecca sighed.

She agreed with every undertone in that puff of air.

"I'll have Pascal bring him back in a few minutes. There's something we need to discuss with both of you." And that little statement screamed of reporting to the principal's office or a *duh-duh-duh* from a movie. Rebecca's red nails tapped on her phone screen. "There. He'll bring him up in ten minutes. Okay, so we never really got to have our social-media talk." She sank into the chair and pulled up something on her phone.

When she turned it around, Sara saw that it was a Twitter page. "I have a million followers on Twitter?"

She'd never made a post.

"Well, you had fifty thousand when we were supposed to meet, then the"—she coughed—"gunshot incident happened, and things sort of grew from there. I've only posted pictures of your artwork here and on Instagram and status updates of your recovery. Nothing specific," she added when Sara started to speak. "Just general things like 'she is okay and healing.' "

Rebecca stopped as Sara scrolled down the feed, half-expecting it to look like her accounts after she'd had the gold medal taken from her.

Oh, the troll comments were there. It *was* the Internet, after all. But, surprisingly, the nastiness was few and far between.

Though one particular trend caught her attention.

"Why do they keep mentioning Mike's mother?" The comments didn't bring up the gun or the attempted abduction. Instead, they kept mentioning collusion and unearthed files.

What was going on?

Rebecca took the phone back and opened Instagram, showing her a profile filled with super cool shots of her artwork interspersed with photos of the city and the team.

"I took a little creative license with this one, reposting some of the official Gold photos—with credit, of course. You've got nearly a million on here too." Rebecca licked her lips. "Now as for Mike's mother—"

The door pushed open, Mike and Pascal stepping through.

"Ah. Perfect timing," Rebecca said. "I was just filling Sara in."

Her gaze flew to Mike's. She could feel the frown pulling her brows together. Mike was paler than she'd ever seen him.

Pascal nudged Mike toward a chair. "Sit. You've had a shock."

"Shock?" Sara asked. Her heart twisted. "What's going on? Why—"

"My mother did it all," Mike said. "Every last bit of it."

He sounded broken, literally shredded inside.

"I—um . . ." She shook her head. "We already knew she released the pictures."

"She did a little more than that," Rebecca said, gently now.

Sara tried to understand. "Well, of course she shot me, but—"

"My mother was responsible for the cheating allegations."

"But—" Her breath left her body as the pieces in her mind began shifting into place. The Twitter comments. And what had Patricia said? That Sara had never realized the connection. Not then. Not now.

"This is a copy of the report from Monique's private investigator. She wanted to apologize for going over your head and hiring him, but I think you'll be glad she did." Rebecca pulled out a file, setting it gently in Sara's lap. "This"—she held up another—"is from Devon's company."

They were each easily a hundred pages long.

"The gist of them is that Mike's mother, Patricia Stewart, met a reporter after you'd won the gold. He wanted the scoop on you, and she was fresh out of rehab, desperate for money and Hydrocodone. They made a deal and fabricated the evidence for the story."

Sara rubbed her head. Fake. She'd known that, but the proof back then—bank statements, the video of her meeting with the judges, her scores—

"My coach told—"

"Unfortunately, your coach had something to hide," Rebecca said. "A criminal record stemming from a rape charge. He technically wasn't allowed to be coaching at all and the reporter took advantage of that."

Sara's eyes closed. It was even more twisted than she could have possibly imagined. She opened, met Rebecca's solid gaze. "So when those first stories broke while I was on tour—the accusations of me paying off the judges—"

"The reporter and his so-called sources."

"And the video?"

"Not you, but you already knew that."

"No. I didn't." Which had been part of the problem. She'd met with so many people during the lead-up and following the competition that Sara *hadn't* been sure if she'd met with the judges or not.

"Well, it's not." Rebecca tapped the report in Sara's lap. "There's a copy of a check in here to an actress who looks remarkably like you, one who admitted that it was her in that video." The publicist made a disgusted sound. "The idiots didn't even use cash."

"I—" Sara shook her head, trying to comprehend everything.

"And that's not even considering the bank accounts. Easy to trace today, much harder to do so years ago."

"My mother." Mike voice was almost toneless, except for the current of regret threading through his words. "The accounts went back to my *mother*."

"It wasn't just the accounts," Rebecca said gently, taking the files back. "None of the sources could hold up today, not with how pervasive technology is. But a decade ago, they were just strong enough to fool anyone who bothered to look."

"And not many people bothered to," Sara said.

Rebecca shook her head. "No, unfortunately, they didn't. Even the IOC only did a slip-shod job of investigating."

Sara had the feeling it wouldn't have mattered if the powers that be at the IOC had found her not guilty of wrong-doing back then. The public—including her parents and friends—had already lost faith in her.

The media might have loved her as a champion, but a fallen cheater was a much better story.

Rebecca slipped the files into her briefcase. "These will be released once you've been discharged, if that's okay with you?"

"No." Sara shook her head. Her redemption wouldn't come from dragging Mike through the mud.

"Yes." Mike's voice was rough, but his eyes were on fire.

"No," she snapped. "It's not me at the expense of you. You need to think about you—"

"My mother *shot* you! She nearly killed you and ruined your life—"

"But *you* didn't." Sara felt tears well in her eyes. "*You didn't.* Now please come here. I can't"—her words hitched—I can't do this without you."

Finally, he came to her, sitting on the edge of the bed. "I'm sorry. I—"

"It hurts," she murmured. "So much."

"What hurts, sweetheart?" Fingers stroked down her cheeks, wiping away the moisture.

"The distance you put between us."

Regret clouded his face. "Shit. I'm fucking this up again, aren't I?"

She sniffed, but the tension that had been invading her body dissipated. "That seems to be your specialty."

Rebecca's phone buzzed, drawing both of their gazes. "Sorry," she muttered. "And apparently, my specialty is ruining romantic moments." Her eyes flicked down to her phone. "And you may not have a choice about those files." She nodded at Pascal. "Turn the TV to Channel Five."

"Why?" Mike asked.

"You're the lead story."

FORTY

Mike

MIKE HELPED Sara maneuver herself from the car. She didn't complain, but her face was gray.

"Put on that suit of armor, Stewart!" one of the paparazzi yelled, "And carry your girl inside."

"Don't you dare," Sara gritted out. "I'm walking into this house on my own two feet."

He waved, ignoring them as he carefully wove his arm around her waist and helped Sara up the front stairs. Here there were only two, compared to the three in the garage, and this door would bring her closer to the bedroom.

"Shit," she muttered taking a halting step. "This fucking hurts."

"More or less than ice burn?"

She paused, considering. "Less, surprisingly." Then she started slowly forward again.

Fuck it.

Moving before she could stop him, Mike wove his arms

around her legs and shoulders and lifted her up against his chest. The paparazzi cheered and catcalled.

"Let me at least get the do—"

The front door opened before she finished her sentence.

Sara sighed and Mike laughed as he carried her inside, kicking the heavy wooden panel closed behind them.

Brit and Monique squealed from the entryway. "You're home!"

"Yup," Sara said dryly. "And so is everyone else." A curly head popped out from behind Monique's legs. Mira was crying. "What is it, honey?" Sara asked.

"You're hurt."

"Not so hurt anymore."

"Then why is Mr. Mike carrying you?" A lip slid out, pouting.

Sara smiled. "Because he's stubborn."

Mira tilted her head, thinking that over. "My mom says that about my dad a lot." Brit stifled a giggle. "Dad says he learned from the best."

They all laughed . . . until Sara groaned and said, "Don't do that. Doesn't hurt except for laughing."

"And walking," Mike muttered.

"And talking," Monique said.

"And breathing," Brit added.

"And . . . playing Legos!" Mira chirped.

They stopped and looked at her, confused. The little girl shrugged. "When I tried to go into my mom's room last night, she said I couldn't because she and dad were playing Legos." There that lip went again. "*I* wanted to play Legos."

"When you're older," Sara deadpanned after they had all unsuccessfully hidden their laughter. "Now, not to ruin the party, but I'm sure Mr. Mike's arms are tired, and I'm done with the damsel-in-distress act."

Monique and Mira shepherded them upstairs, Brit trailing behind. They got her settled in the bed, covered in blankets and Netflix-cued-up with *The Crown*.

Gentle hugs followed, and Mike walked the girls down. Brit hesitated in the threshold of the front door after Monique had walked off with Mira.

"Pascal gave this to Rebecca to give to—" She shook her head and set Sara's engagement ring into the palm of his hand. "They took it off for surgery and wanted to keep it safe, I guess."

Mike held up the ring, watching the emeralds glitter in the afternoon light. "If I was a better man, I'd leave her to her life. Let her start over."

"If you were a coward, maybe," Brit said. "You guys have history . . . some really shitty pieces of it. But there are also the good times, and I think that if you can get past the guilt, you'll realize those outweigh all the bad."

He thought of those mornings with Sara years ago, punctuated with laughter and private jokes. He thought of her in his bed, feeling the soft, warm weight of her body against his. Her smile. Her scent. Her kind soul and kick-ass attitude.

There just wasn't any way that he could live without her.

She made his life complete.

Brit clapped him on the shoulder. "And know that she's thinking of those good times too. That she doesn't blame you for your mom. That she's more worried about how *you* were hurt from it all."

"That's fucked up."

A shrug. "That's love. You put the other person's feelings first," Brit said. "So don't bother martyring yourself when it will only piss off your woman."

He snorted.

"You know it's true."

Shaking his head, he waved at Brit as she headed for her car, then turned to close the door.

"Play Miley for her," she called. "Girls dig Miley."

"You have terrible taste in music!" he yelled.

"I'm still faster."

Mike closed the door and bounded up the stairs. Sara was in his bed, color returning to her cheeks as she sipped from a water bottle.

"Don't play me Brit's music, okay?"

He blinked. She pointed . . . at the open window.

"You heard?"

"Yup." She patted the bed next to her. "Brit gives pretty solid advice, music excluded."

Mike crossed the room and carefully slid onto the mattress next to her. "I don't know what's going to happen with my mom."

"Me neither."

"I want her to go to jail." He tucked the blankets more securely around her. "She needs to pay somehow."

One-half of Sara's mouth curved. "I'm not opposed to the jail scenario. But I'm not going to worry about it. We've got good lawyers. I'm going to let them fight that battle for me."

She sighed when he nodded.

"What?"

"You haven't kissed me." His face scrunched up, she elaborated. "Since the . . . incident, you haven't kissed me."

He thought, and well . . . damn, he *hadn't* kissed her. Not more than a peck on the forehead at least. He waggled his brows. "Think I should remedy that?"

A smirk. "Maybe."

"Maybe means yes."

"In this case"—one of her hands slid to the back of his head and tugged—"maybe means yes."

Then his lips were on hers, and nothing else mattered. Not his mom. Not the press. Not the team.

Just him and her.

"I love you," he said and held up the ring. "Will you marry me . . . again I guess?"

"I will marry you so hard you won't know what hit you."

He grinned and slipped the band on her finger. "Bring it. I can take whatever you dish out, Sara girl."

FORTY-ONE

Six Months Later

Sara

"AGAIN," Sara said, "but this time bend your knee more on the landing."

She watched as Mira skated away and then back toward her, launching herself into a Salchow. The girl wobbled but stayed on her feet.

"Yes! Way to go!"

Mira hugged her around the waist. "Can I can play with my friends now?"

"Heck yeah."

With a laugh, Sara moved to the boards. Mira had talent but perhaps not the interest or drive for competitive skating. In the meantime, Sara was just teaching her a bit here and there.

She reached for a tissue, but a hand—a very familiar one—grabbed the box before she got there.

"You aren't going to wipe it for me too?" she teased when Mike held it out for her.

"Shush, you." He leaned over the boards and kissed her. "Want company?"

She glanced down, saw he had his skates on. "Isn't this a little too tame for you?" It was just public skating, no pucks or sticks in sight.

"You're about all I can handle."

One leg then the other slid over the dasher and onto the ice. Mike laced her fingers with his. "You okay with the verdict?"

His mom had taken a plea deal—twenty years to life for attempted murder and a variety of other charges the lawyers had filed. Sara would be lying if she said that she was unhappy.

After all his mother had done to Mike and then hurting Pascal, not to mention the whole *shooting* her and ruining her life thing, forever would be too soon to see Patricia Stewart again.

"Yup, I'm good with it."

"Good." He grinned. "So you going to set a date for our wedding any time soon?"

The running joke between them made her smile. Mike was ready to make things official. She thought since they'd gotten betrothed so quickly that a long engagement wouldn't hurt.

"Nope."

"I'd like our honeymoon to not be interrupted by training camp," he grumbled.

Mira flew past them, laughing like the little lunatic she was.

"Or we can just start our honeymoon tonight," she said, seeing Mitch walk into the rink. He nodded at her.

It was time.

Mike frowned. "What are you talking about?"

"Funny thing is"—she paused when Coach Bernard skated up to them—"I always thought I'd get married at center ice."

Mike's headed flipped back and forth between her and Coach. "No dress?"

She grinned, ran her free hand down her sweatshirt and leggings. "No dress." She pointed at a white swirl on her thigh. "This is enough white, don't you think?"

Mike nodded, his face grave. "Are you serious right now?"

Stefan and Brit skated over. Stefan had the rings, Brit a small bouquet of flowers.

Spence and Monique slowly made their way toward them, Monique wobbling like a baby deer as Spence basically held her up.

"You owe me a really freaking great party after all this," Monique grumbled. "I'm made for heels, not skates."

Sara laughed. "Deal." She nodded at Bernard, who she was only just starting to know. Brit, apparently, had goaded him into getting his officiate paperwork.

Then she turned to the love of her life, grabbed his hand, and tugged him toward center ice. "Ready to start that happily ever after, Hot Shot?"

EPILOGUE

Mandy

"LESS MUGGLES, MORE MAGIC," Mandy murmured as she scrolled through her *Harry Potter* Pinterest board, trying to find the perfect themed appetizers for the movie marathon she was hosting that weekend. She knew she was unreasonably excited about having a party at her new apartment, but this was big.

As in the apartment was the biggest purchase she had ever made.

Smiling, she leaned back in her chair and continued scrolling through her phone. A hockey game was playing in the background, the volume low enough that the announcers' voices were a muted hum. But that didn't matter, she would hear if anything exciting happened, the crowd's cheers would radiate through the concrete layers of the arena to where her office was situated.

Mandy always joked that her office was Harry's equivalent of his closet bedroom—a tiny cubbyhole in the bowels of the

Gold Mine, the home rink for the NHL's newest team, the San Francisco Gold.

Her office might be small, but the physical therapy space certainly wasn't.

A half dozen treatment tables were set up in the large room outside her door, each complete with their own built-in cabinets filled to the brim with the best supplies money could buy.

The PT suite tended to be one of the hubs—players always coming in and out, lots of activity, voices, laughter—for her team, second only to the space where they relaxed, ate, played video games, or binged the latest hit on Netflix.

But for the most part, Mandy loved all the activity. She enjoyed the players crossing through to access the weight room, or take a dip in the pool, or soak their aching muscles in the hot and cold tubs. And with the team's doctor, masseuse, and other support therapy staff's own small offices surrounding hers, it was hardly ever quiet.

Except now.

While the doctor and his assistant were rink side—near the team in case anyone got injured—the rest of the training staff had gone to grab a bite. She'd stayed behind this time, nibbling on a salad and taking advantage of the mental break by blissfully scrolling through wand-shaped appetizers on her phone.

After the final buzzer, the activity would ramp up again. The players each had their own post-game routines—maybe a massage or a soak in the icy, cold tub, usually some time spent on the exercise bike, slowly cooling their muscles after the strenuous sixty-minute game.

As for her?

Her phone and those magical treats would lay forgotten because she'd be running around like a chicken without its head.

Multiple players would need different treatments, and it was her job to coordinate with the masseuse and the doctor to assess injuries old and new, advise beneficial exercises and stretches, and . . .

She spent most of her time trying to pretend that Blane was just another player.

"Idiot," she muttered as just his name conjured up all sorts of very unprofessional images into her mind.

Muscles.

The kind that made the spot just below her belly button clench with need.

Strong legs and, good gravy, but his ass.

Hockey players had the *best* asses.

No pancake bottoms, these men—and *women*—could fill out a pair of jeans. She wanted to squeeze it, to nibble it, bounce a dime—

Mandy dropped her chin to her chest, losing sight of the Sorting Hat cupcakes she'd been pondering.

Blane with his yummy ass had a unique way of distracting her.

No, it wasn't even distraction, per se. He had *always* been able to get under her skin.

And that was very, very bad for her.

"Ugh," she said, tossing her phone onto her desk and standing, knowing that she wouldn't be able to sit still now.

Nope, she needed about forty laps in the pool and a good hard fu—

Run, her mind blurted, almost yelling at the mental voice of her inner devil. *A good hard run.*

Unfortunately, the cajoling tone wasn't completely drowned out. *Some sexy horizontal time with Blane would be more fun—*

But the rest of the enticing words were lost as the roar of the crowd suddenly penetrated through the layers of concrete. Her stomach twisted. Mandy could tell, even before her eyes made it to the television, that it wasn't in celebration of a goal or a good hit either.

This was fury, a collective of outrage.

She was on her feet the moment she saw the prone form lying so still face down on the ice.

Her gut twisted when she spotted the curving line of a numeral two on the back of the player's jersey.

"Not him," she said and the words were familiar, a sentiment she had whispered, had *prayed* a thousand times before. She needed the camera angle to shift, for her to be able to see more clearly *who* was hurt. "Not him."

Then Dr. Carter was on the ice and the player moved slightly, rolling away from the camera, giving a full shot of his back and the matching twos adorning his jersey.

Fuck. Not him. Not Blane.

And that was when she saw the pool of blood.

—Get Boarding, Book 3 of the Gold Hockey series, now available.

GOLD HOCKEY SERIES

Blocked

Backhand

Boarding

Benched

Breakaway

Breakout

Checked

GOLD HOCKEY

Did you miss any of the Gold Hockey books?
Find information about the full series here.
Or keep reading for a sneak peek into each of the books below!

Blocked
Gold Hockey Book #1
Get your copy at books2read.com/Blocked

Brit

THE FIRST QUESTION Brit always got when people found out she played ice hockey was *"Do you have all of your teeth?"*

The second was *"Do you, you know, look at the guys in the locker room?"*

The first she could deal with easily—flash a smile of her full set of chompers, no gaps in sight. The second was more problematic. Especially since it was typically accompanied by a smug smile or a coy wink.

Of course she looked. *Everybody* looked once. Everyone

snuck a glance, made a judgment that was quickly filed away and shoved deep down into the recesses of their mind.

And she meant *way* down.

Because, dammit, she was there to play hockey, not assess her teammates' six packs. If she wanted to get her man candy fix, she could just go on social media. There were shirtless guys for days filling her feed.

But that wasn't the answer the media wanted.

Who cared about locker room dynamics? Who gave a damn whether or not she, as a typical heterosexual woman, found her fellow players attractive?

Yet for some inane reason, it *did* matter to people.

Brit wasn't stupid. The press wanted a story. A scandal. They were desperate for her to fall for one of her teammates—or better yet the captain from their rival team—and have an affair that was worthy of a romantic comedy.

She'd just gotten very good at keeping her love life—as nonexistent as it was—to herself, gotten very good at not reacting in any perceptible way to the insinuations.

So when the reporter asked her the same set of questions for the thousandth time in her twenty-six years, she grinned—showing off those teeth—and commented with a sweetly innocent "Could've sworn you were going to ask me about the coed showers." She waited for the room-at-large to laugh then said, "Next question, please."

–Get your copy at books2read.com/Blocked

Backhand
Gold Hockey Book #2
Get your copy at books2read.com/Backhand

Sara

"Sorry I messed up your sketch," he rumbled.

She nibbled on the side of her mouth, biting back a smile. "Sorry I stole your hand for so long."

He shrugged. "My mom's an artist. I get it."

Well, there went her battle with the smile. Her lips twitched and her teeth came out of hiding. If there was one thing that Sara had, it was her smile. It had been her trademark in her competition days.

Which were long over.

Her mouth flattened out, the grin slipping away. Time to go, time to forget, to move on, to rebuild. "Thanks," she said and extended a hand.

Then winced and dropped it when her ribs cried out in protest.

"You okay?" he asked, head tilting, eyes studying her.

"Fine." And out popped her new smile. The fake one. Careful of her aching side, she shrugged into her backpack. "I've got to go." She turned, ponytail flapping through the hair to land on her opposite shoulder.

"That—" He touched her arm. "Wait. I *know* I know you."

She froze. That was the second time he'd said that, and now they were getting into dangerous territory. Recognition meant . . . no. She couldn't.

There had been a time when *everyone* had known her. Her face on Wheaties boxes, her smile promoting toothpaste and credit cards alike.

That wasn't her life any longer.

"Thanks again. Bye." She started to hurry away.

"Wait." A hand dropped on to her shoulder, thwarting her escape, and she hissed in pain.

"Sorry," he said, but he didn't release her. Instead, he shifted his grip from her aching shoulder down to her elbow and when she didn't protest, he exerted gentle pressure until Sara was facing him again. "It's just that know I *know* you."

No. This wasn't happening.

"You're Sara Jetty."

Her body went tense.

Oh God. This was *so* happening.

"It's me." He touched his chest like she didn't know he was talking about himself, and even as she was finally recognizing the color of his eyes, the familiar curve of his lips and line of his jaw, he said the worst thing ever, "Mike Stewart."

Oh *shit*.

—Get your copy at books2read.com/Backhand

Boarding
Gold Hockey Book #3
Get your copy at books2read.com/Boarding

HOCKEY PLAYERS HAD the *best* asses.

No pancake bottoms, these men—and *women*—could fill out a pair of jeans. She wanted to squeeze it, to nibble it, bounce a dime—

Mandy dropped her chin to her chest, losing sight of the Sorting Hat cupcakes she'd been pondering.

Blane with his yummy ass had a unique way of distracting her.

No, it wasn't even distraction, per se. He had *always* been able to get under her skin.

And that was very, very bad for her.

"Ugh," she said, tossing her phone onto her desk and standing, knowing that she wouldn't be able to sit still now.

Nope, she needed about forty laps in the pool and a good hard fu—

Run, her mind blurted, almost yelling at the mental voice of her inner devil. *A good hard run.*

Unfortunately, the cajoling tone wasn't completely drowned out. *Some sexy horizontal time with Blane would be more fun—*

But the rest of the enticing words were lost as the roar of the crowd suddenly penetrated through the layers of concrete. Her stomach twisted. Mandy could tell, even before her eyes made it to the television, that it wasn't in celebration of a goal or a good hit either.

This was fury, a collective of outrage.

She was on her feet the moment she saw the prone form lying so still face down on the ice.

Her gut twisted when she spotted the curving line of a numeral two on the back of the player's jersey.

"Not him," she said and the words were familiar, a sentiment she had whispered, had *prayed* a thousand times before. She needed the camera angle to shift, for her to be able to see more clearly *who* was hurt. "Not him."

Then Dr. Carter was on the ice and the player moved slightly, rolling away from the camera, giving a full shot of his back and the matching twos adorning his jersey.

Fuck. Not him. Not Blane.

And that was when she saw the pool of blood.

—Get your copy at books2read.com/Boarding

Benched

Gold Hockey Book #4

Get your copy at books2read.com/Benched

Max

He started up the car, listening and chiming in at the right places as Brayden talked all things video game.

But his mind was unfortunately stuck on the fact that women were not to be trusted.

He snorted. Brit—the Gold's goalie and the first female in the NHL—and Mandy—the team's head trainer—would smack him around for that sentiment, so he silently amended it to: *most* women were not to be trusted.

There. Better, see?

Somehow, he didn't think they'd see.

He parked in the school's lot, walked Brayden in, and received the appropriate amount of scorn from the secretary for being thirty minutes late to school, then bent to hug Brayden.

"I'll pick you up today," he said.

Brayden smiled and hugged him tightly. Then he whispered something in his ear that hit Max harder than a two-by-four to the temple.

"If you got me a new mom, we wouldn't be late for school."

"Wh-what?" Max stammered.

"Please, Dad? Can you?"

And with that mind fuck of an ask, Brayden gave him one more squeeze and pushed through the door to the playground, calling, "Love you!" over his shoulder.

Then he was gone, and Max was standing in the office of his son's school struggling to comprehend if he had actually just heard what he'd heard.

A new mom?

Fuck his life.

—Get your copy at books2read.com/Benched

Breakaway

Gold Hockey Book #5
Get your copy at books2read.com/BreakawayGold

Blue

"Thanks for the ride."

"Try not to go out and get a fresh bimbo to ride tonight. I hear STIs on are the rise in the city."

Blue sighed, turned back to face her. "Really?"

She shrugged, smirk teasing the edges of her mouth, drawing his focus to the lushness of her lips. "Just watching out for Max's teammate."

He rolled his eyes. "Not hardly."

"Okay, how about I'm trying to prevent you from spreading STIs to the female populace."

"I'm clean, and I'm smart," he told her. "Condoms all the way."

"Ew."

Except there was something about the way she said it that made Blue stiffen and take notice. Because . . . he stared into her eyes, watched as the pale blue darkened to royal, saw her lips part, and her suck in a breath.

Holy shit.

"You're attracted to me."

Her jaw dropped. "No fucking way," she said, too quickly, pink dancing on the edges of her cheekbones. "You're delusional."

Blue got close.

Real close.

Anna licked her lips.

And fuck it all, he kissed that luscious mouth.

—Breakaway, www.books2read.com/BreakawayGold

Breakout

Gold Hockey Book #6

Get your copy at books2read.com/Breakout

PR-Rebecca

A fucking perfect hockey fairy tale.

Shaking her head, because she knew firsthand that fairy tales didn't exist outside of rom-coms and occasionally between alpha sports heroes and their chosen mates, Rebecca slipped through the corridor and stepped onto the Gold's bench.

Lots of dudes in suits—of both the boardroom *and* the hockey variety—were hugging.

On the ice. Near the goals. On the bench.

It was a proverbial hug-fest.

And she was the cynical bitch who couldn't enjoy the fact that the team she was with had just won the biggest hockey prize of them all.

"I knew you'd be like this."

Rebecca turned her focus from Brit, who was skating with the huge silver cup, to the man—no, to the *boy* because no matter how pretty and yummy he was, Kevin was still a decade younger than her—leaning oh so casually against the boards.

"Nice goal," she told him.

A shrug. "Blue made a nice pass."

And dammit, the fact that he wasn't an arrogant son of a bitch made her like him more.

She nodded at the cup. "You should go have your turn."

"I'll get mine," he said with another shrug.

She frowned, honestly confused. "You don't want—"

Suddenly he was in front of her on the bench, towering over her even though she was wearing her four-inch power heels. "You know what I want?"

Rebecca couldn't speak. Her breath had whooshed out of her in the presence of all that sweaty, hockey god-ness. Fuck he was pretty and gorgeous and . . . so fucking masculine that her thighs actually clenched together.

She wanted to climb him like a stripper pole.

"Do you?" he asked again when her words wouldn't come. "Want to know what I want?"

She nodded.

He bent, lips to her ear. "You, babe," he whispered. "I. Want. You."

Then he straightened and jumped back onto the ice, leaving her gaping after him like she had less than two brain cells in her skull.

The worst part?

She wanted him, too.

Had wanted him since the moment she'd laid eyes on the sexy as sin hockey god.

"Trouble," she murmured. "I'm in *so* much fucking trouble."

—Breakout, www.books2read.com/breakout

Checked
Gold Hockey Book #7
Get your copy at books2read.com/Checked

"Rebecca."

She kept walking.

She might work with Gabe, but she sure as heck wasn't on speaking terms with him. He'd dismissed her work, ignored her contribution to the team. He'd made her feel small and unimportant and—

She kept walking.

"*Rebecca*."

Not happening. Her car was in sight, thank fuck. She beeped the locks, reached for the handle.

He caught her arm.

"Baby—"

"I am *not* your baby, and you don't get to touch me." She ripped herself free, started muttering as she reached for the handle of her car again. "You don't even like me."

He stepped close, real close. Not touching her, not pushing the boundary she'd set, and yet he still got really freaking close. Her breath caught, her chin lifted, her pulse picked up. "That. Is. Where. You're. Wrong."

She froze.

"What?"

His mouth dropped to her ear, still not touching, but near enough that she could feel his hot breath.

"I like you, Rebecca. Too fucking much."

Then he turned and strode away.

—Checked, coming March 29th, 2020, www. books2read.com/Checked

ALSO BY ELISE FABER

Roosevelt Ranch Series (all stand alone, series complete)

Disaster at Roosevelt Ranch

Heartbreak at Roosevelt Ranch

Collision at Roosevelt Ranch

Regret at Roosevelt Ranch

Desire at Roosevelt Ranch

Billionaire's Club (all stand alone)

Bad Night Stand

Bad Breakup

Bad Husband

Bad Hookup

Bad Divorce

Bad Fiancé

Bad Boyfriend (Jan 19th 2020)

Gold Hockey (all stand alone)

Blocked

Backhand

Boarding

Benched

Breakaway

Breakout

Checked (March 29th, 2020)

Chauvinist Stories

Bitch (Feb 16th, 2020)

Cougar (March 1st, 2020)

Whore (March 15th, 2020)

Life Sucks Series (all stand alone)

Train Wreck

Phoenix Series

Phoenix Rising

Dark Phoenix

Phoenix Freed

Phoenix: LexTal Chronicles (rereleasing soon, stand alone, Phoenix world)

From Ashes

KTS Series

Fire and Ice (Hurt Anthology, stand alone)

ABOUT THE AUTHOR

USA Today bestselling author, Elise Faber, loves chocolate, Star Wars, Harry Potter, and hockey (the order depending on the day and how well her team -- the Sharks! -- are playing). She and her husband also play as much hockey as they can squeeze into their schedules, so much so that their typical date night is spent on the ice. Elise is the mom to two exuberant boys and lives in Northern California. Connect with her in her Facebook group, the Fabinators or find more information about her books at www.elisefaber.com.

f facebook.com/elisefaberauthor

a amazon.com/author/elisefaber

BB bookbub.com/profile/elise-faber

o instagram.com/elisefaber

g goodreads.com/elisefaber

p pinterest.com/elisefaberwrite